ROBOT FRENZY

By Erik Craddock

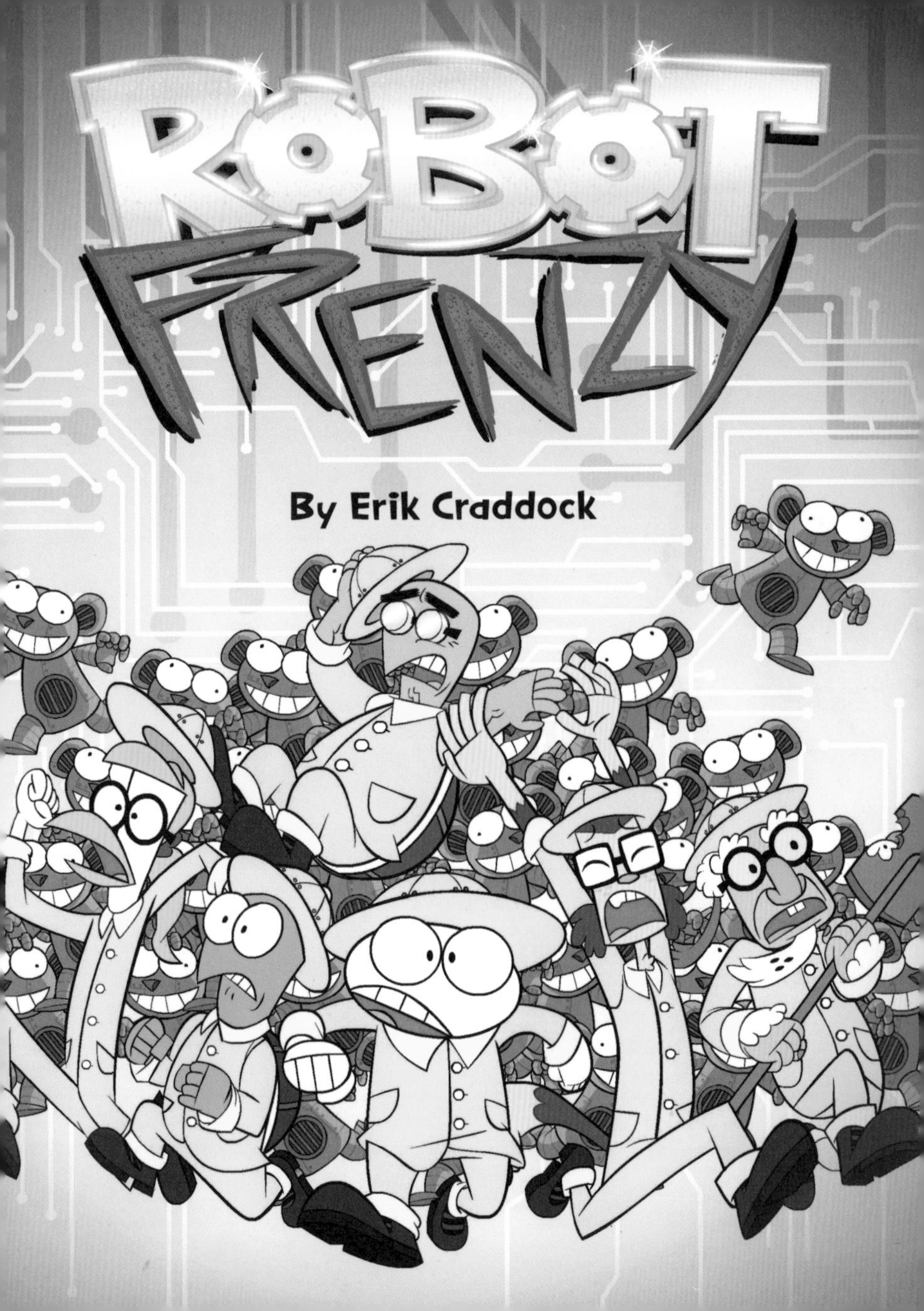

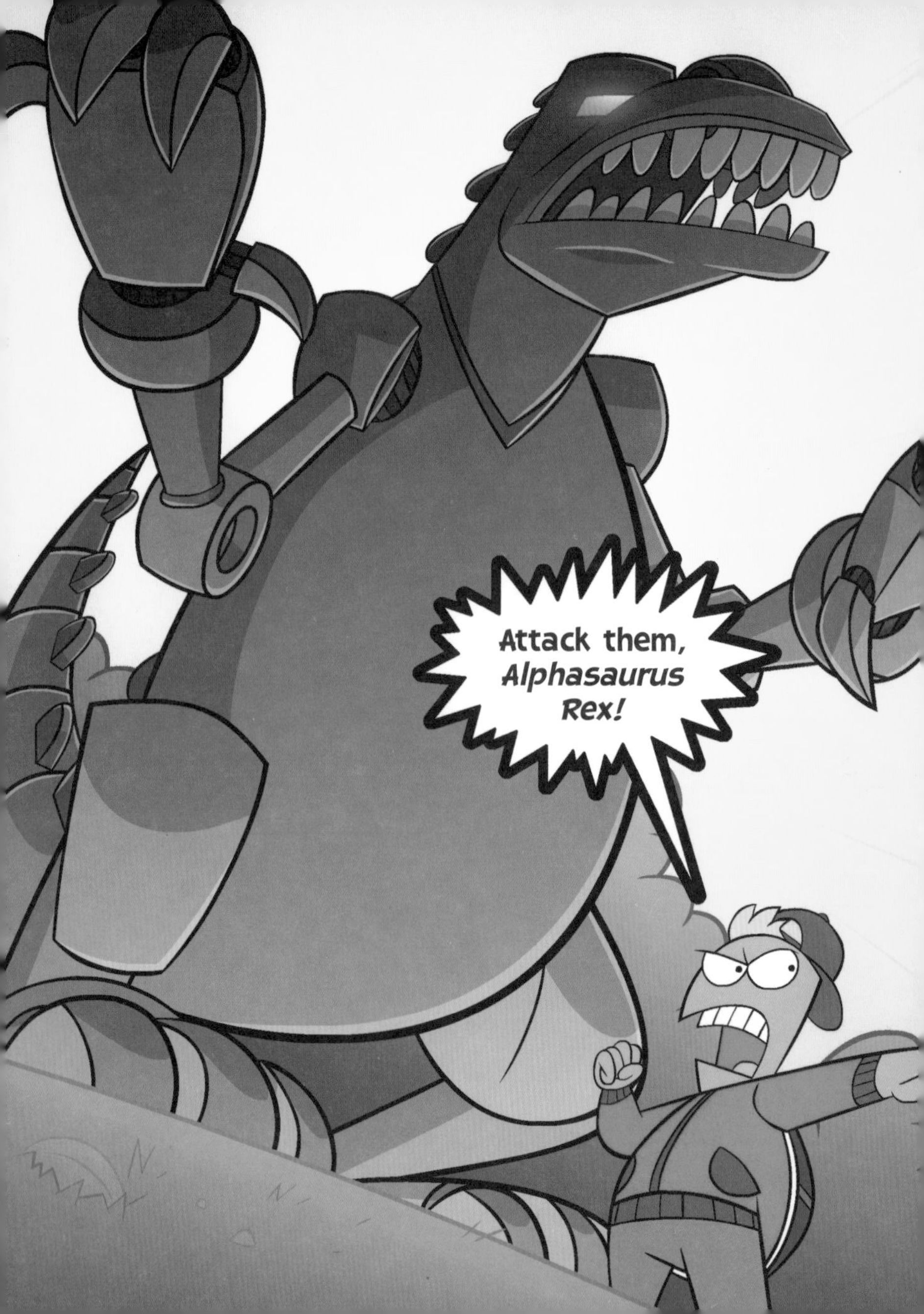
Attack them, Alphasaurus Rex!

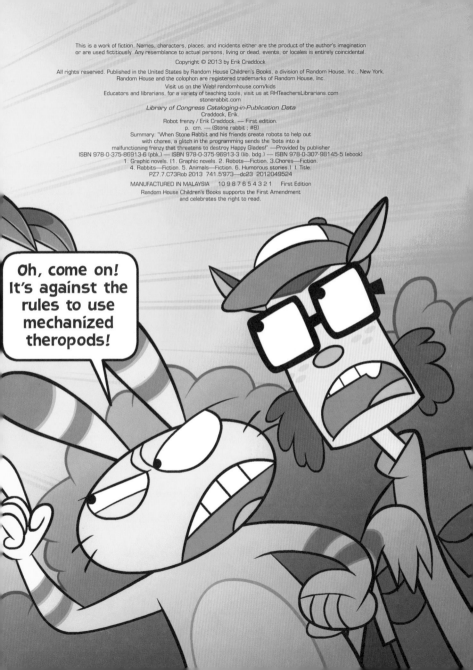

Published in the United States by Random House Children's Books, a division of Random House, Inc., New York.
Random House and the colophon are registered trademarks of Random House, Inc.

Visit us on the Web! randomhouse.com/kids
Educators and librarians, for a variety of teaching tools, visit us at RHTeachersLibrarians.com
stonerabbit.com

Library of Congress Cataloging-in-Publication Data
Craddock, Erik.
Robot frenzy / Erik Craddock. — First edition.
p. cm. — (Stone rabbit ; #8)
Summary: "When Stone Rabbit and his friends create robots to help out with chores, a glitch in the programming sends the 'bots into a malfunctioning frenzy that threatens to destroy Happy Glades!" —Provided by publisher
ISBN 978-0-375-86913-6 (pbk.) — ISBN 978-0-375-96913-3 (lib. bdg.) — ISBN 978-0-307-98145-5 (ebook)
1. Graphic novels. [1. Graphic novels. 2. Robots—Fiction. 3.Chores—Fiction.
4. Rabbits—Fiction. 5. Animals—Fiction. 6. Humorous stories.] I. Title.
PZ7.7.C73Rob 2013 741.5'973—dc23 2012049524

MANUFACTURED IN MALAYSIA 10 9 8 7 6 5 4 3 2 1 First Edition

Random House Children's Books supports the First Amendment
and celebrates the right to read.

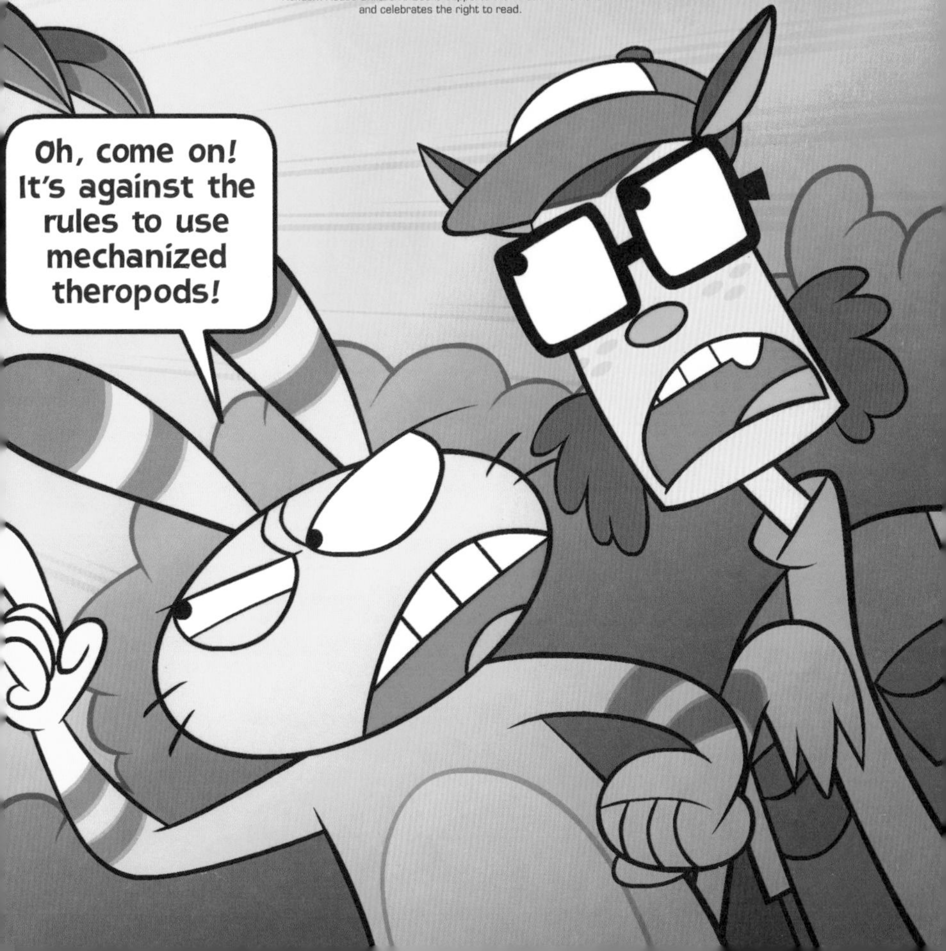
Oh, come on! It's against the rules to use mechanized theropods!

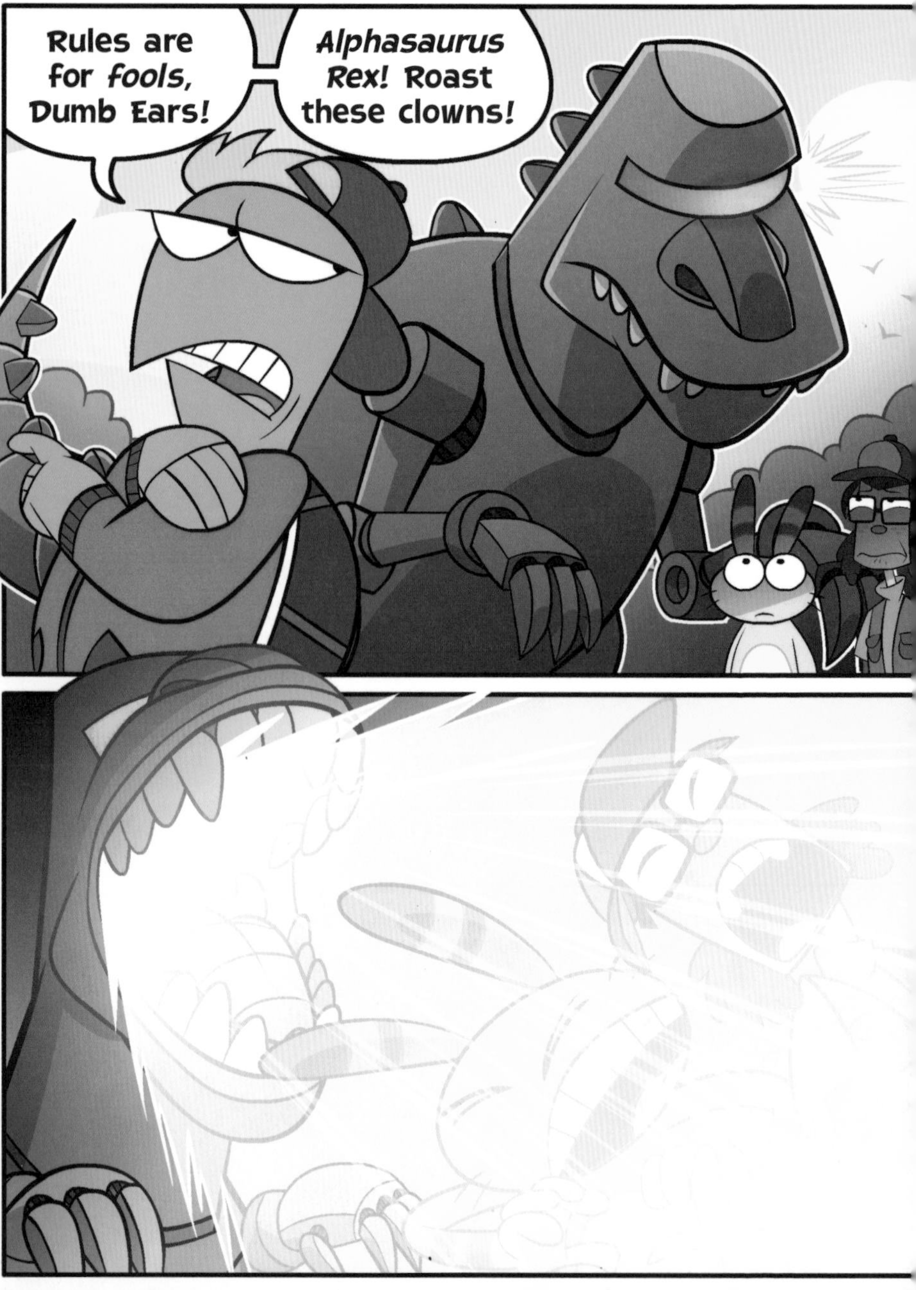
Rules are for *fools*, Dumb Ears!
Alphasaurus Rex! Roast these clowns!

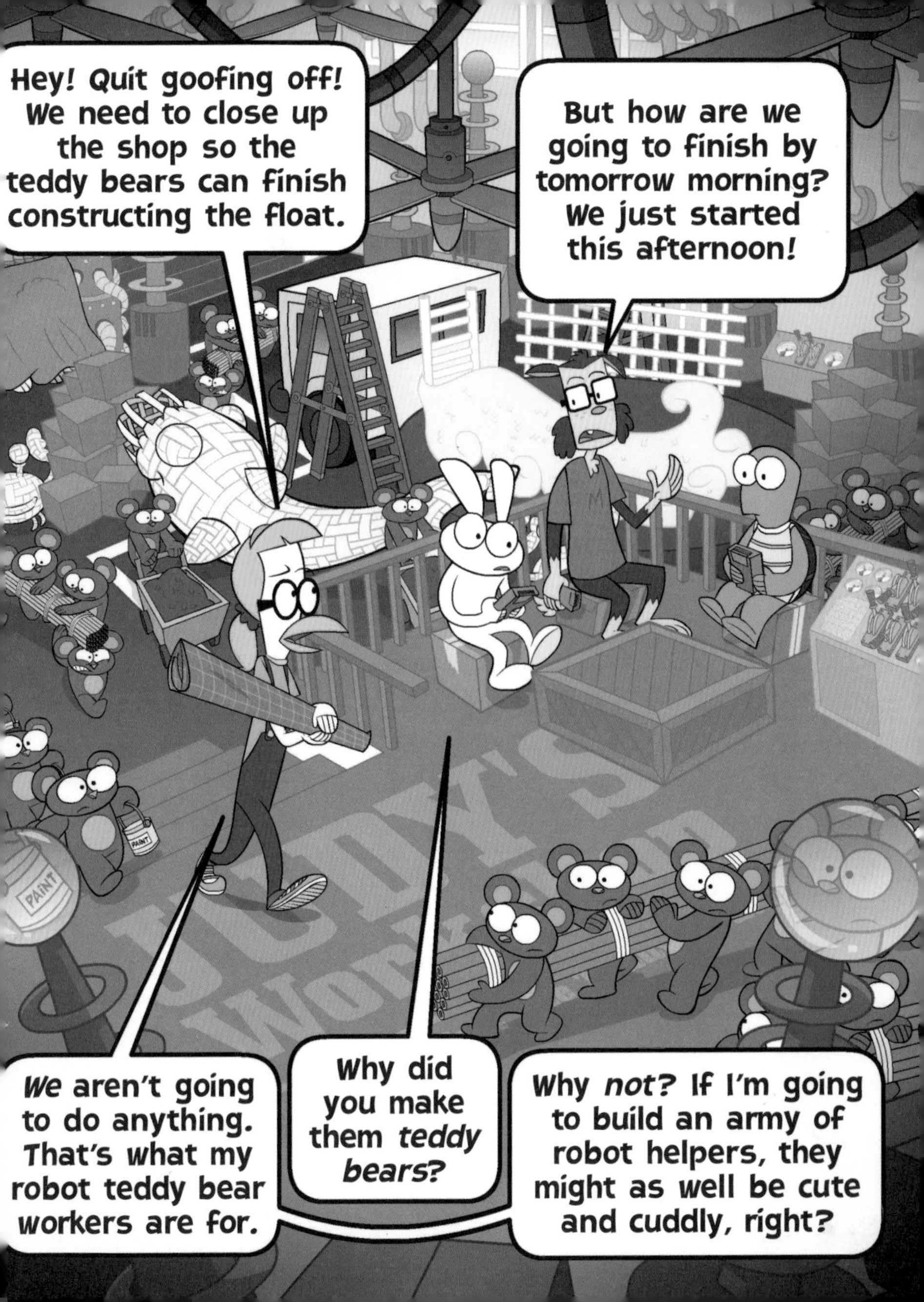
Hey! Quit goofing off! We need to close up the shop so the teddy bears can finish constructing the float.
But how are we going to finish by tomorrow morning? We just started this afternoon!
We aren't going to do anything. That's what my robot teddy bear workers are for.
Why did you make them *teddy bears?*
Why *not?* If I'm going to build an army of robot helpers, they might as well be cute and cuddly, right?

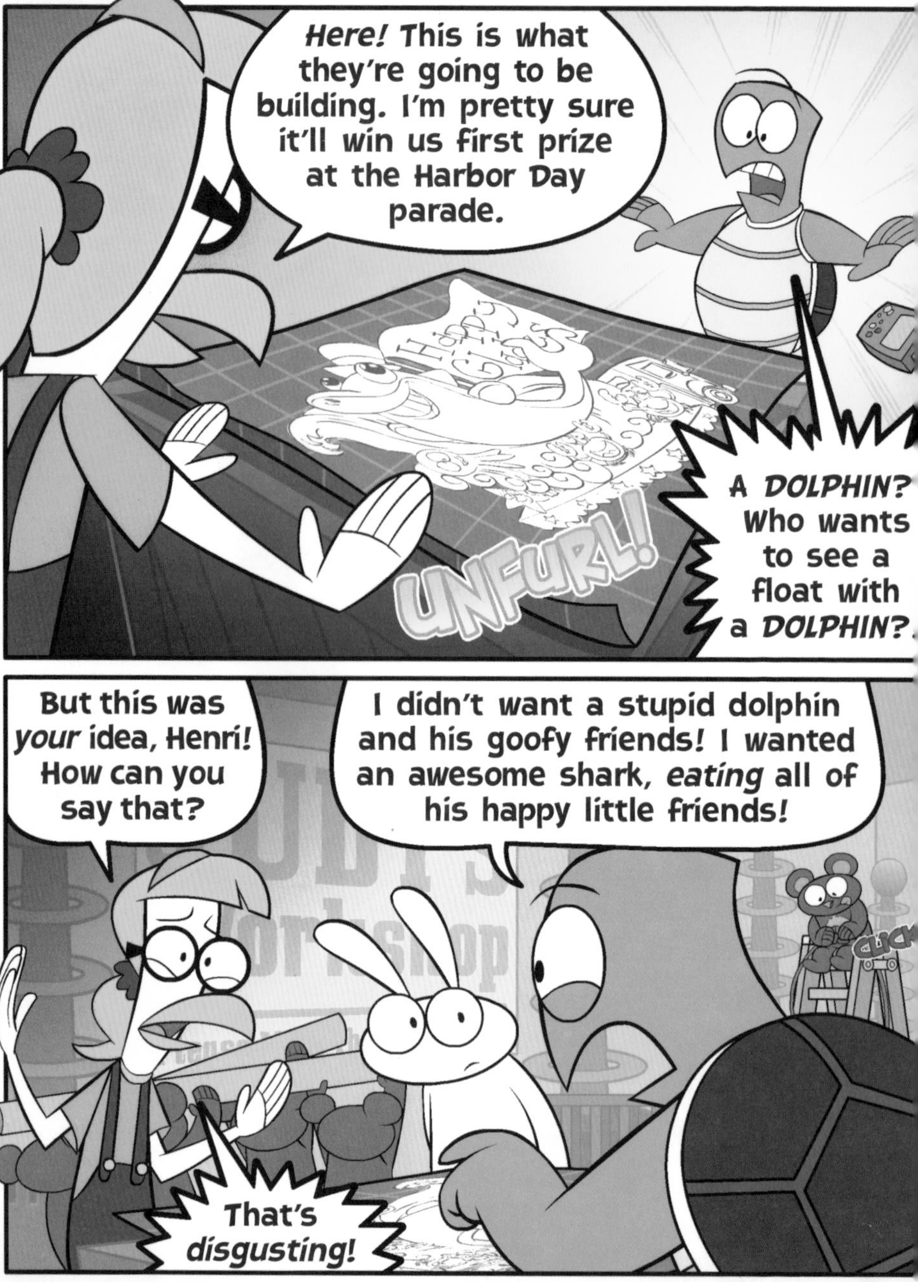

Here! This is what they're going to be building. I'm pretty sure it'll win us first prize at the Harbor Day parade.
UNFURL!
A *DOLPHIN?* Who wants to see a float with a *DOLPHIN?*
But this was *your* idea, Henri! How can you say that?
I didn't *want* a stupid dolphin and his goofy friends! I wanted an awesome shark, *eating* all of his happy little friends!
That's *disgusting!*
CLICK

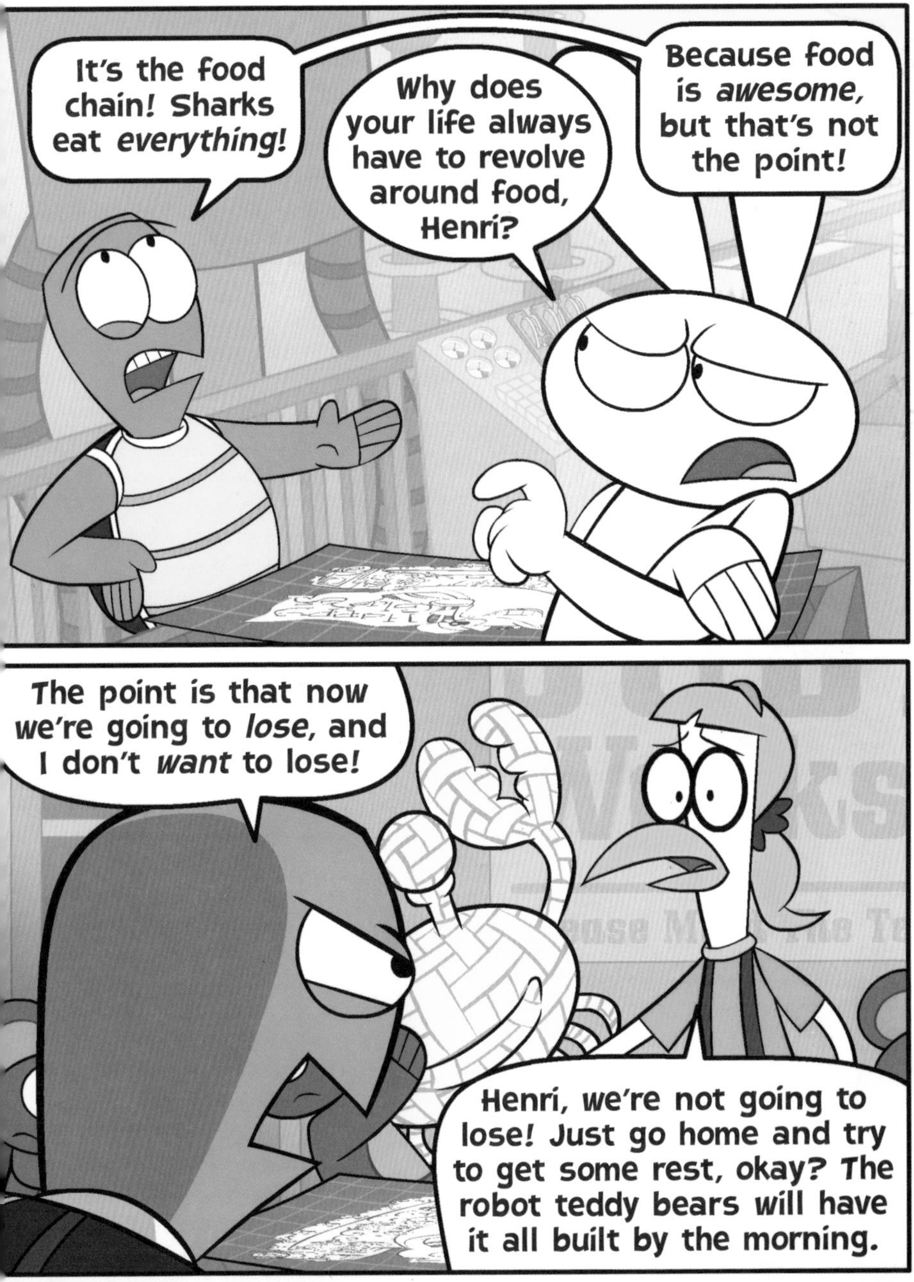
It's the food chain! Sharks eat *everything*!
Why does your life always have to revolve around food, Henri?
Because food is *awesome*, but that's not the point!
The point is that now we're going to *lose*, and I don't *want* to lose!
Henri, we're not going to lose! Just go home and try to get some rest, okay? The robot teddy bears *will* have it all built by the morning.

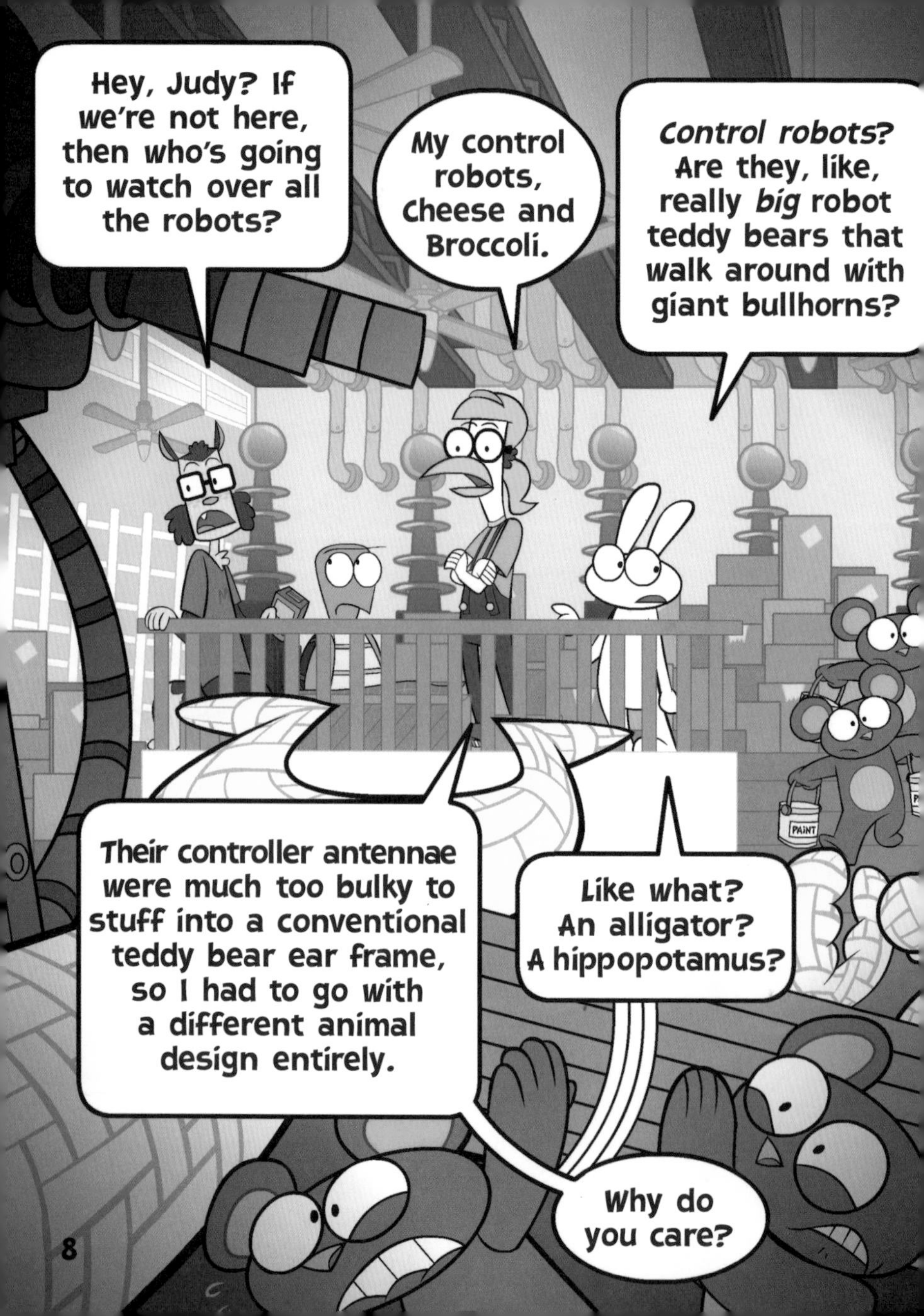
Hey, Judy? If we're not here, then who's going to watch over all the robots?
My control robots, Cheese and Broccoli.
Control robots? Are they, like, really *big* robot teddy bears that walk around with giant bullhorns?
Their controller antennae were much too bulky to stuff into a conventional teddy bear ear frame, so I had to go with a different animal design entirely.
Like what? An alligator? A hippopotamus?
Why do you care?
PAINT

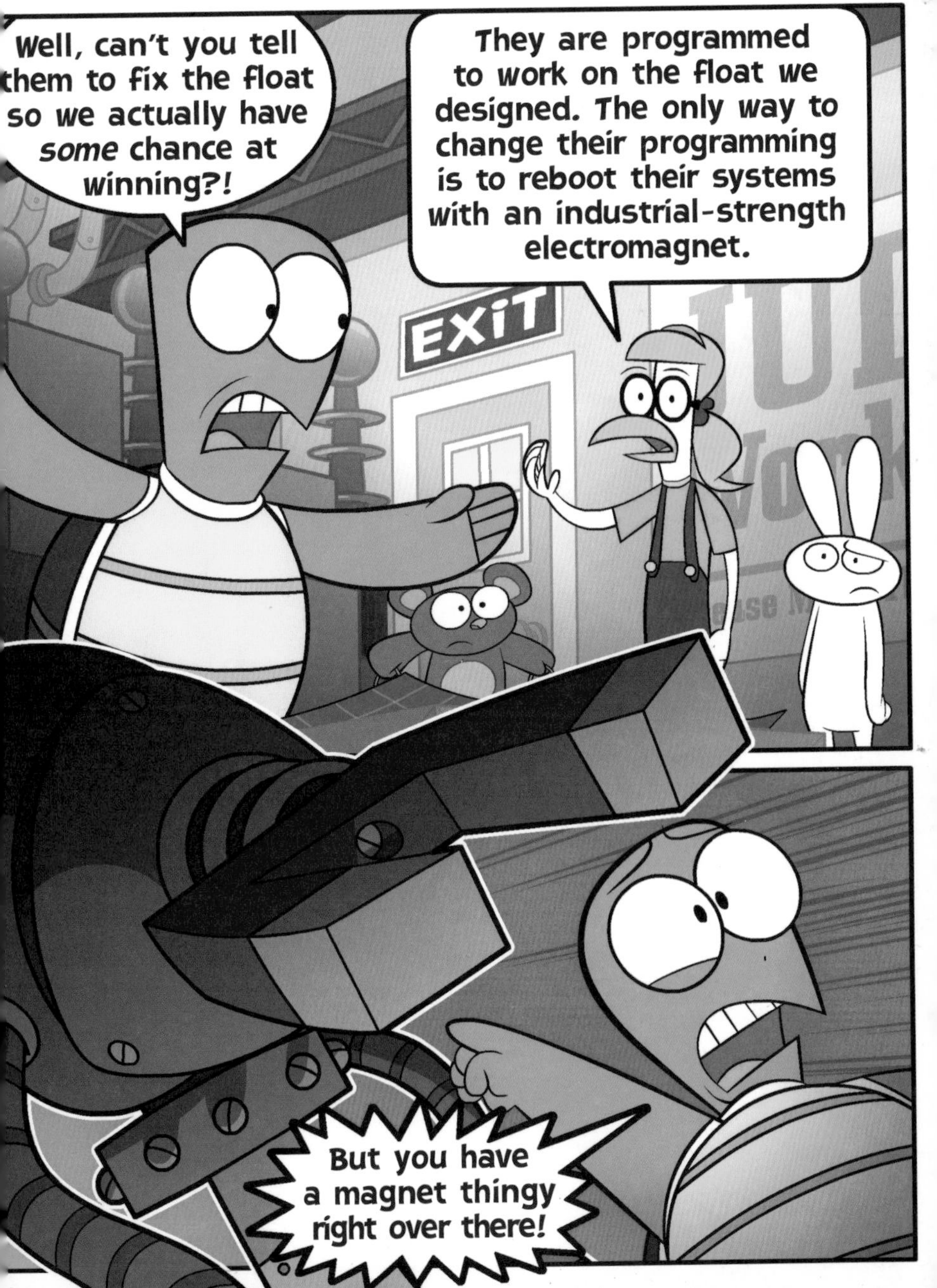
Well, can't you tell them to fix the float so we actually have *some* chance at winning?!
They are programmed to work on the float we designed. The only way to change their programming is to reboot their systems with an industrial-strength electromagnet.
EXIT
But you have a magnet thingy right over there!

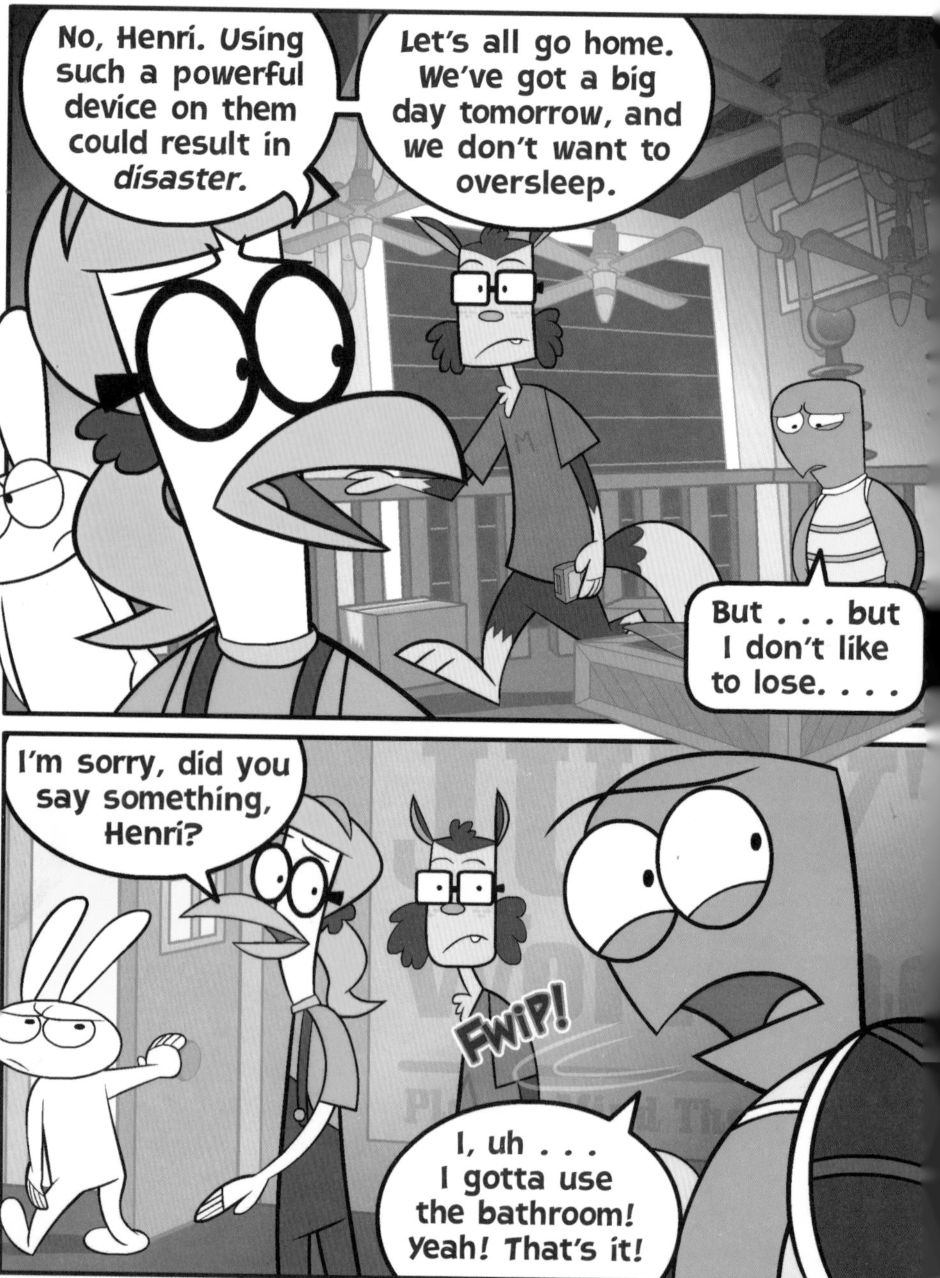
No, Henri. Using such a powerful device on them could result in *disaster*.
Let's all go home. We've got a big day tomorrow, and we don't want to oversleep.
But . . . but I don't like to lose. . . .
I'm sorry, did you say something, Henri?
FWIP!
I, uh . . . I gotta use the bathroom! Yeah! That's it!

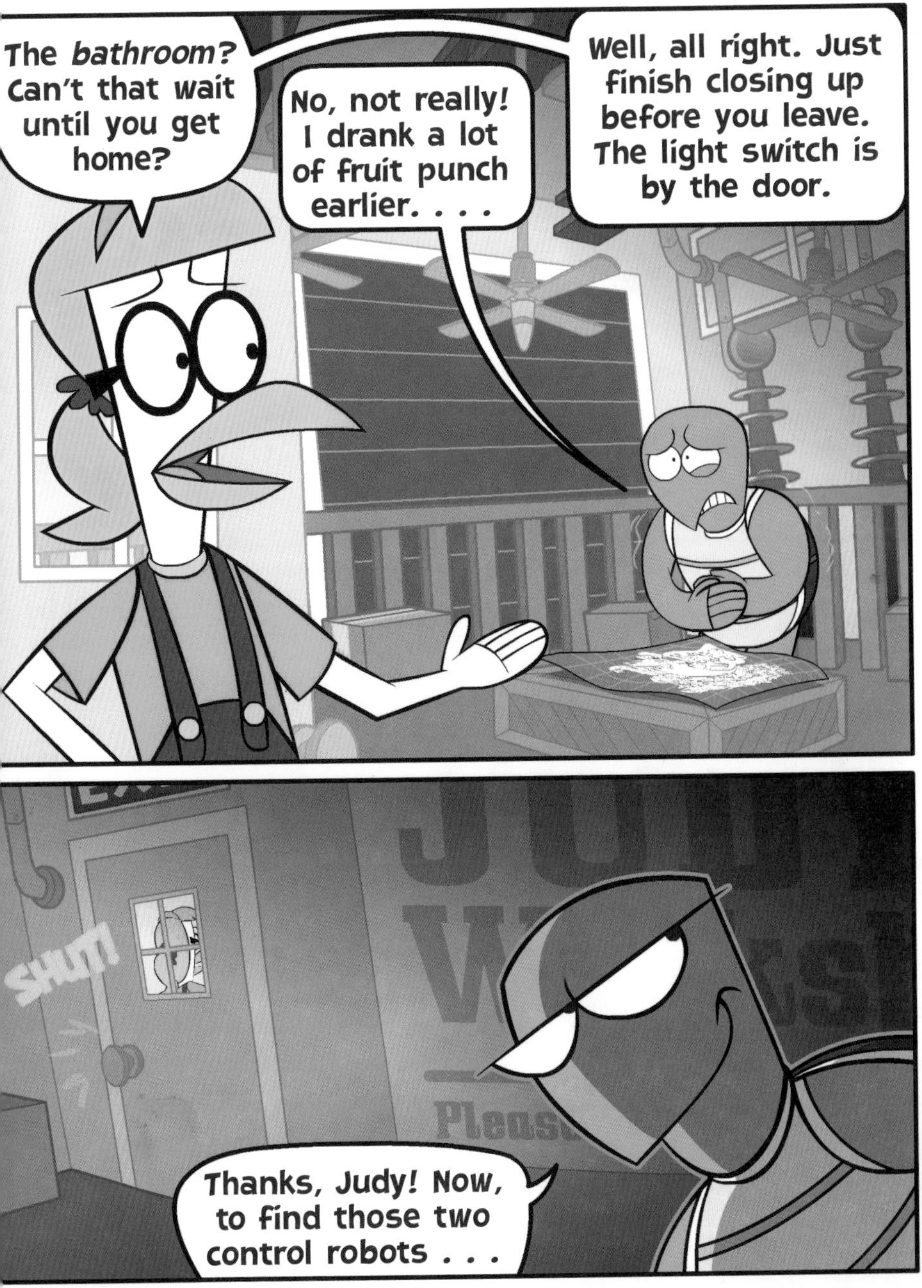
The *bathroom*? Can't that wait until you get home?
No, not really! I drank a lot of fruit punch earlier. . . .
Well, all right. Just finish closing up before you leave. The light switch is by the door.
SHUT!
Thanks, Judy! Now, to find those two control robots . . .

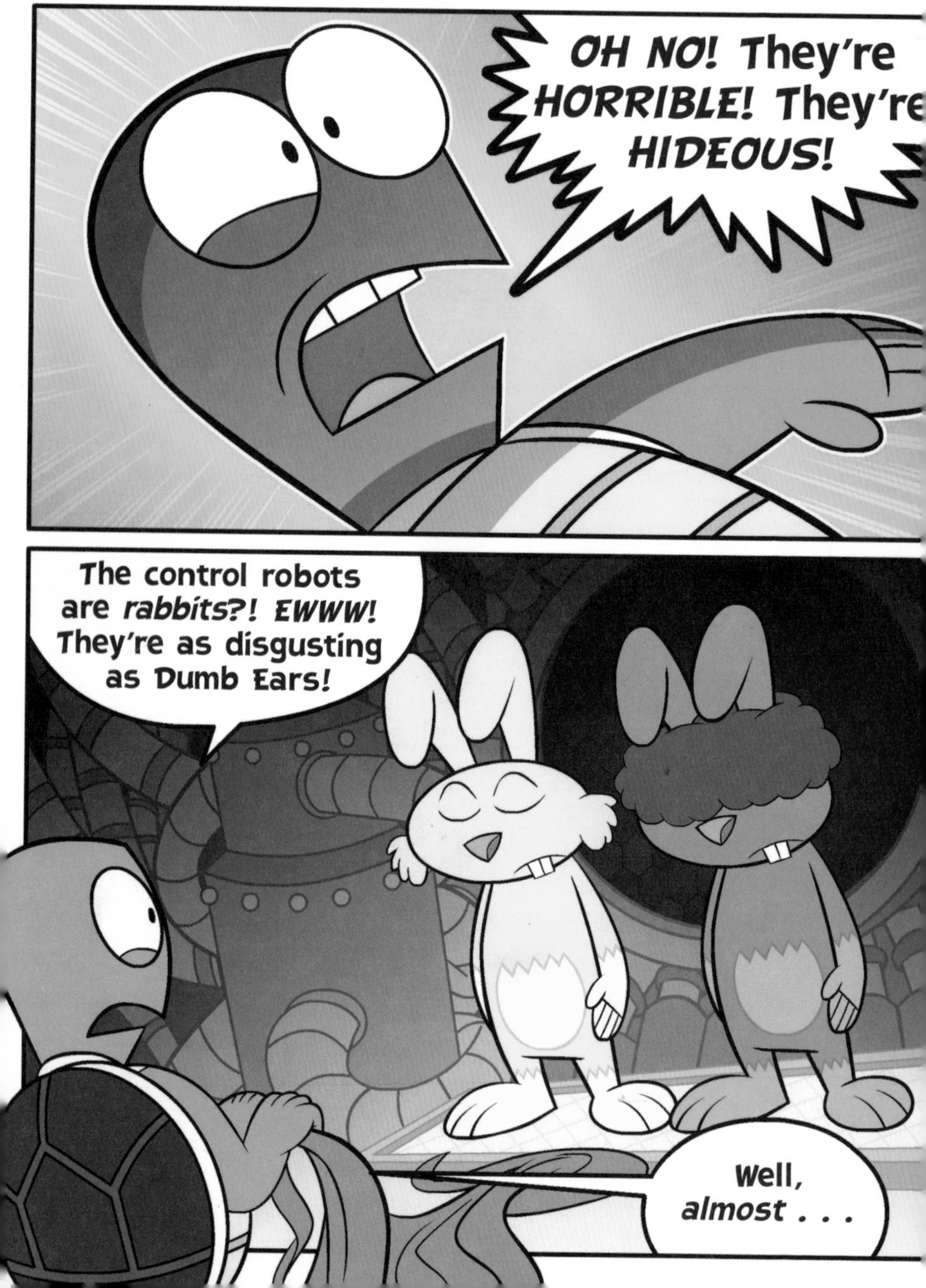
OH NO! They're HORRIBLE! They're HIDEOUS!
The control robots are *rabbits*?! *EWWW!* They're as disgusting as Dumb Ears!
Well, *almost . . .*

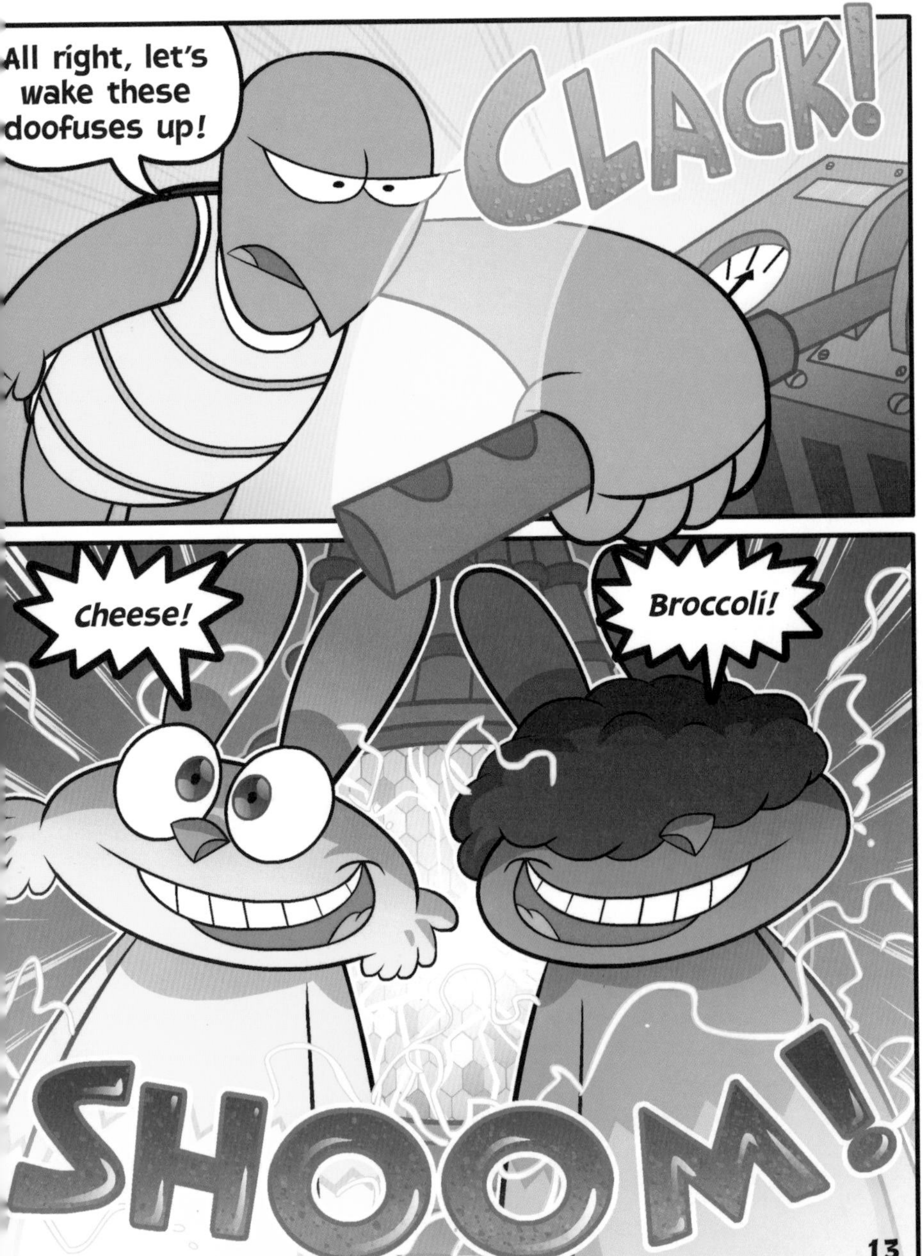
All right, let's wake these doofuses up!
CLACK!
Cheese!
Broccoli!
SHOOM!

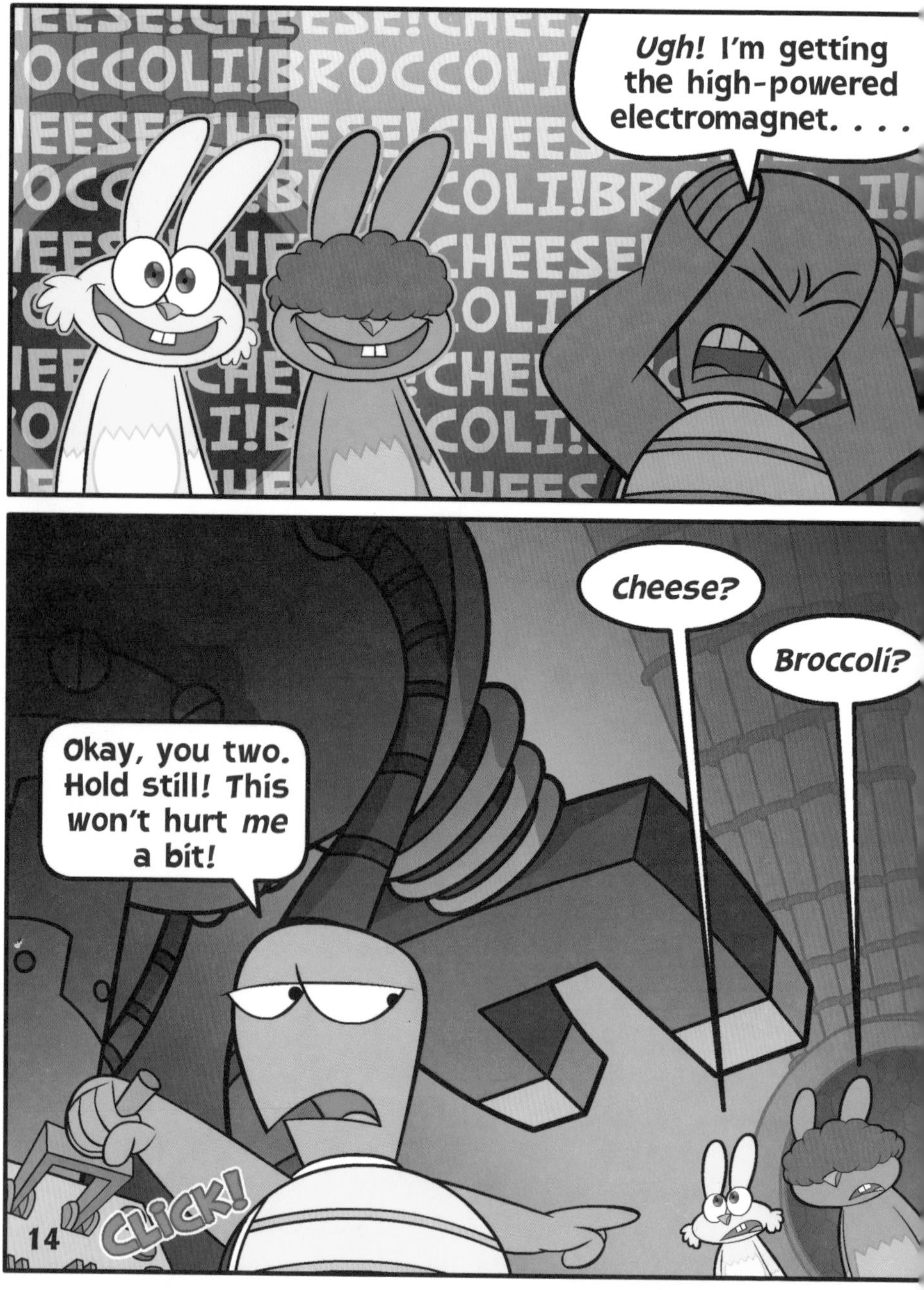
CHEESE!CHEESE!CHEE
OCCOLI!BROCCOLI
Ugh! I'm getting the high-powered electromagnet. . . .
Cheese?
Broccoli?
Okay, you two. Hold still! This won't hurt me a bit!
CLICK!

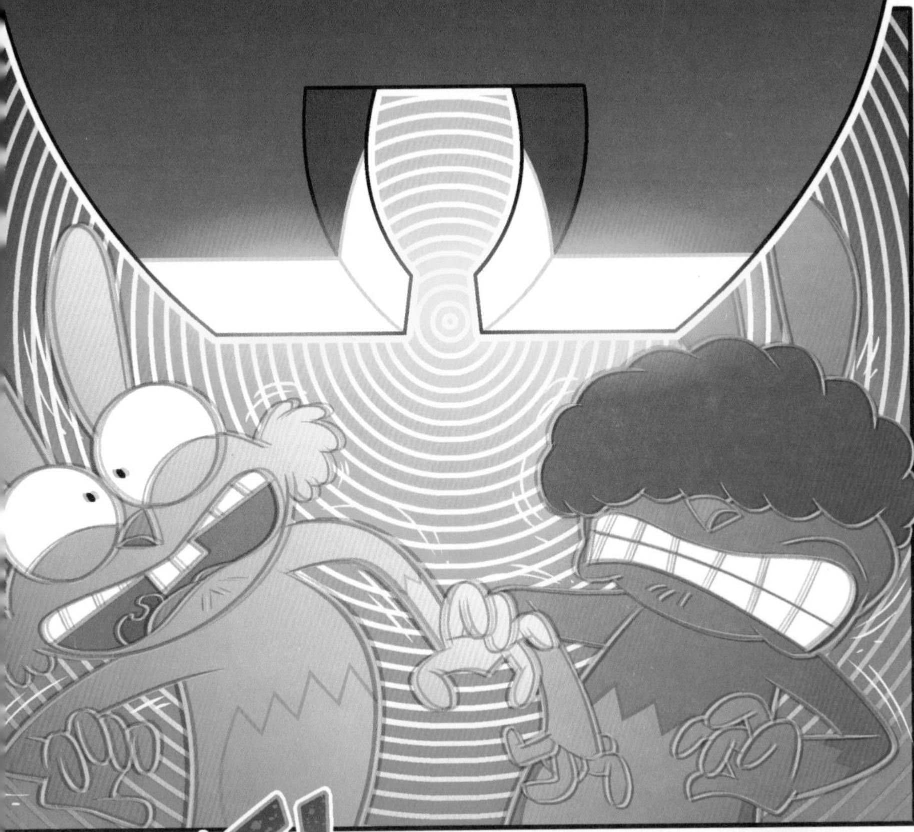

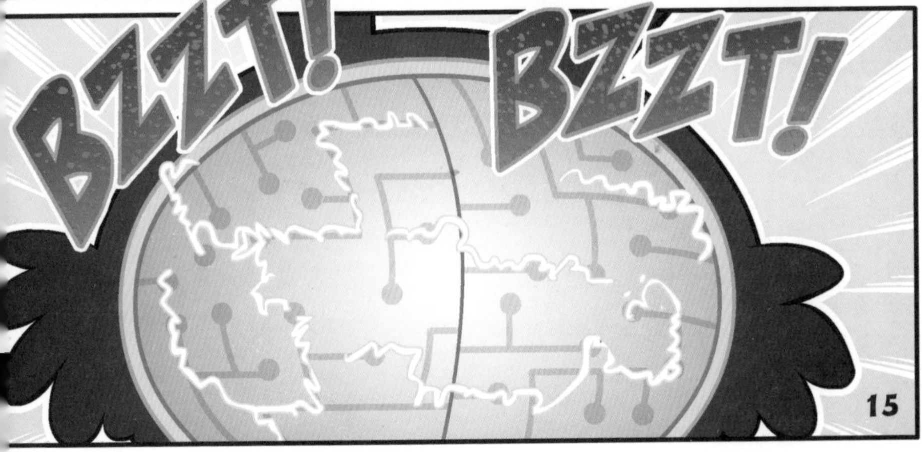
BZZT! BZZT!

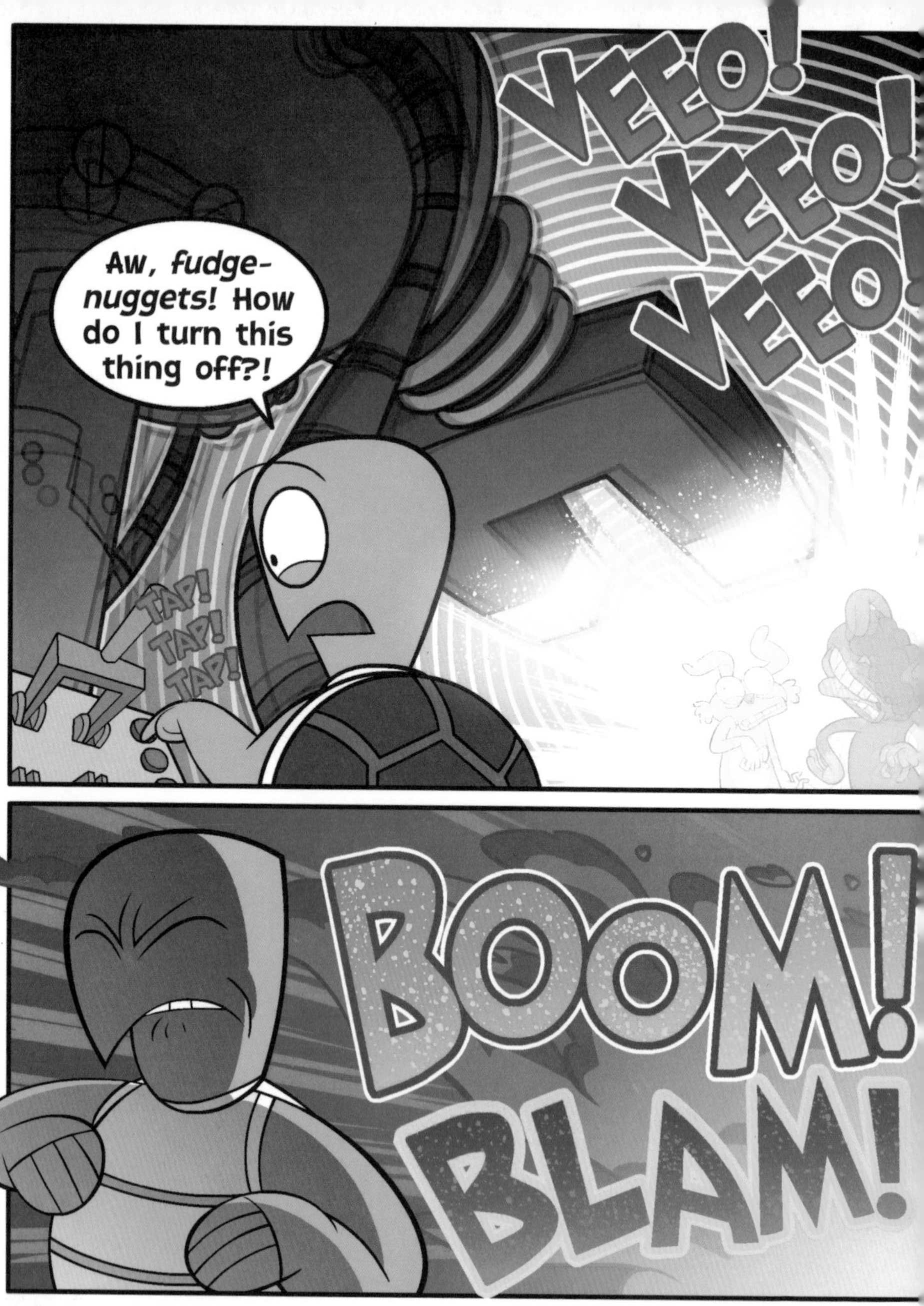
VEEO! VEEO! VEEO!
Aw, fudge-nuggets! How do I turn this thing off?!
TAP! TAP! TAP!
BOOM!
BLAM!

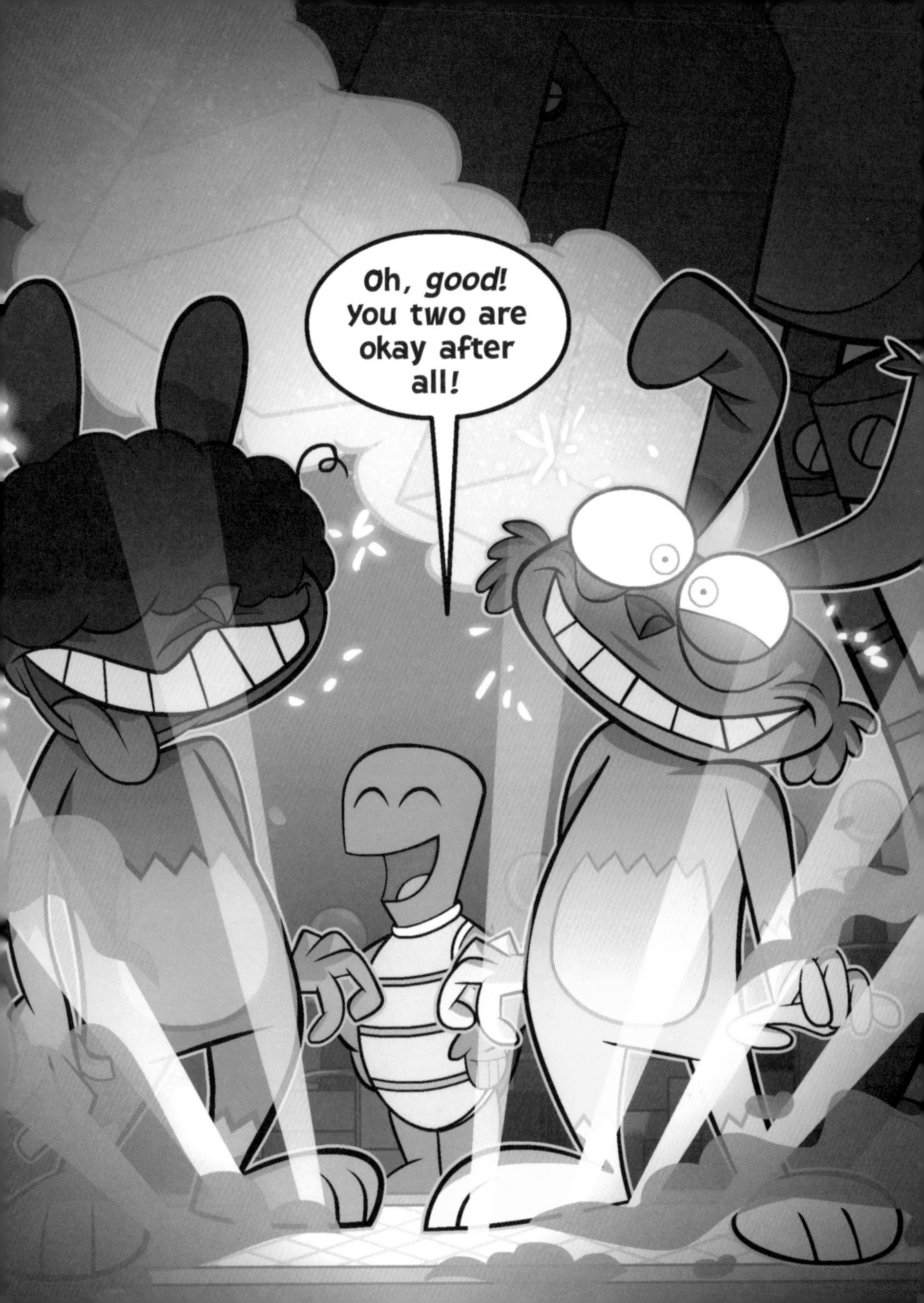
Oh, *good*! You two are okay after all!

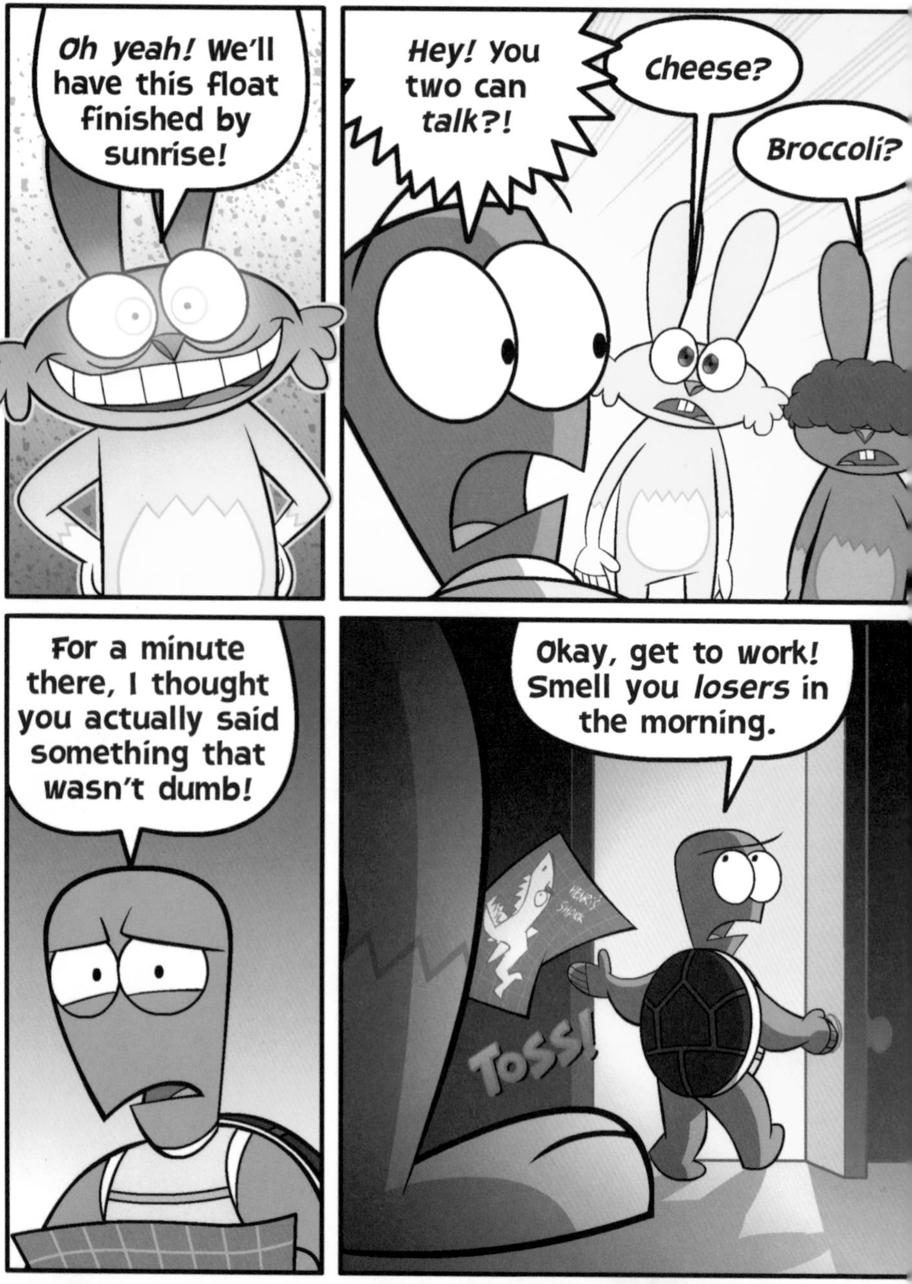

Oh yeah! We'll have this float finished by sunrise!
Hey! You two can talk?!
Cheese?
Broccoli?
For a minute there, I thought you actually said something that wasn't dumb!
Okay, get to work! Smell you losers in the morning.
TOSS!

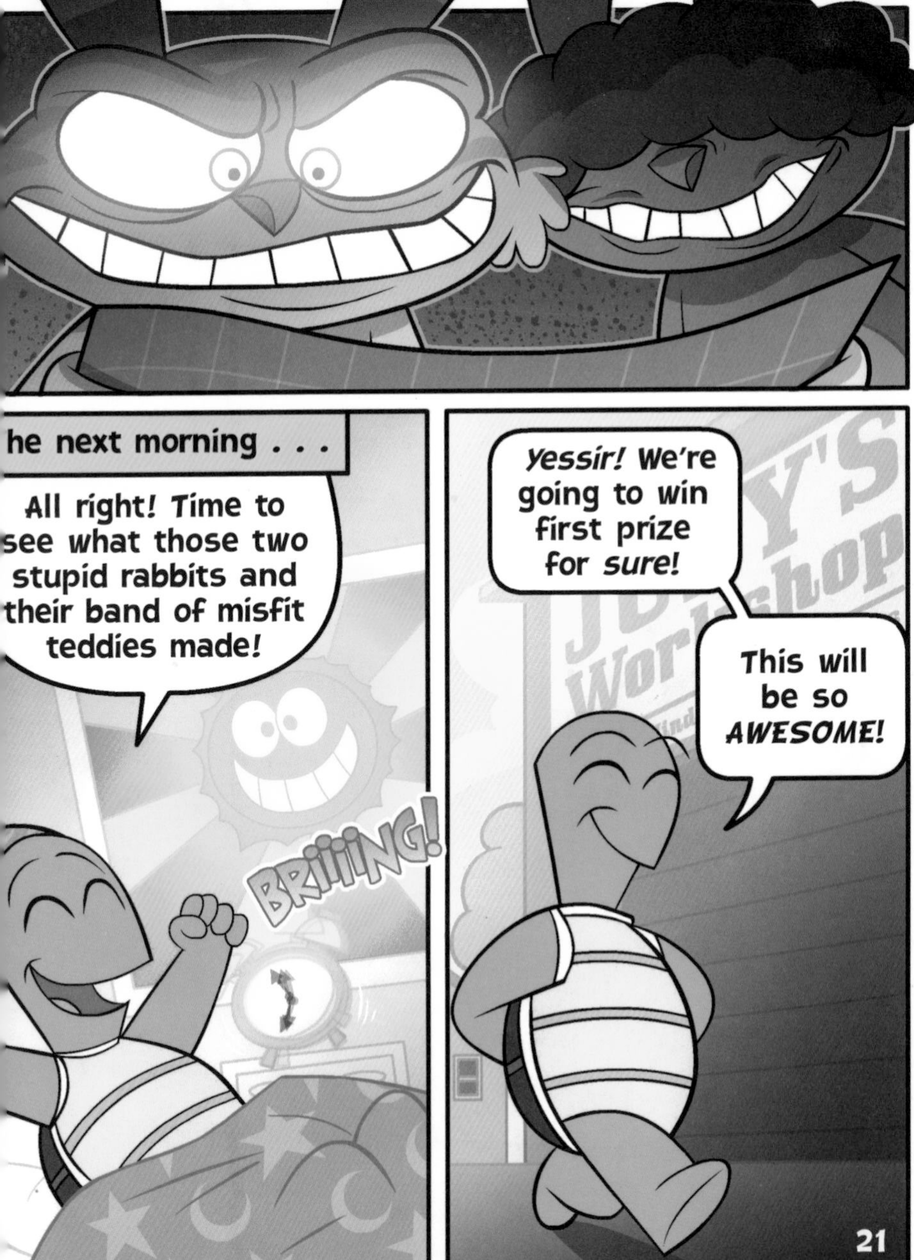

he next morning . . .
All right! Time to see what those two stupid rabbits and their band of misfit teddies made!
BRIIIING!
Yessir! We're going to win first prize for sure!
This will be so AWESOME!

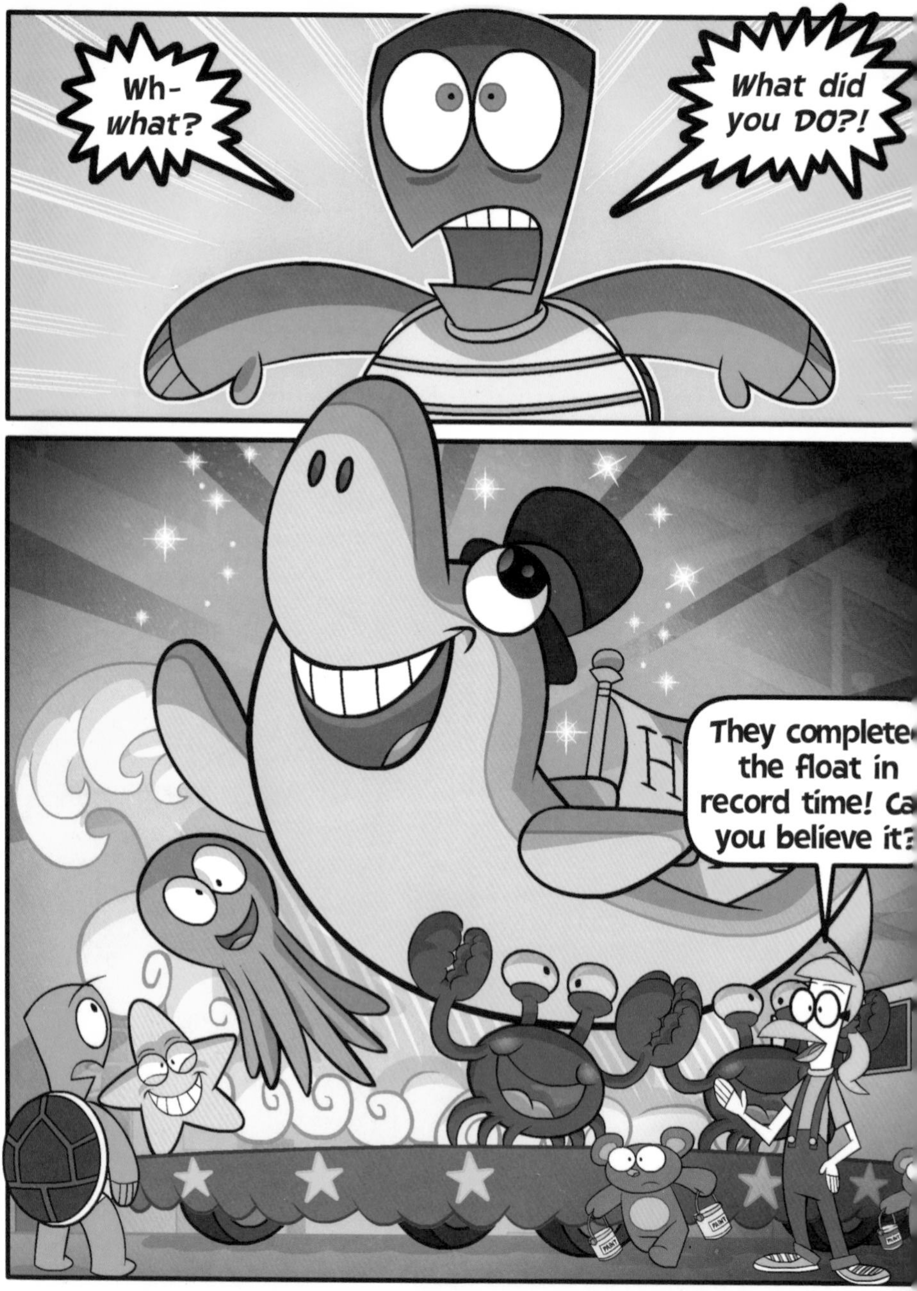
Wh- what?
What did you DO?!
They complete the float in record time! Ca you believe it?

23

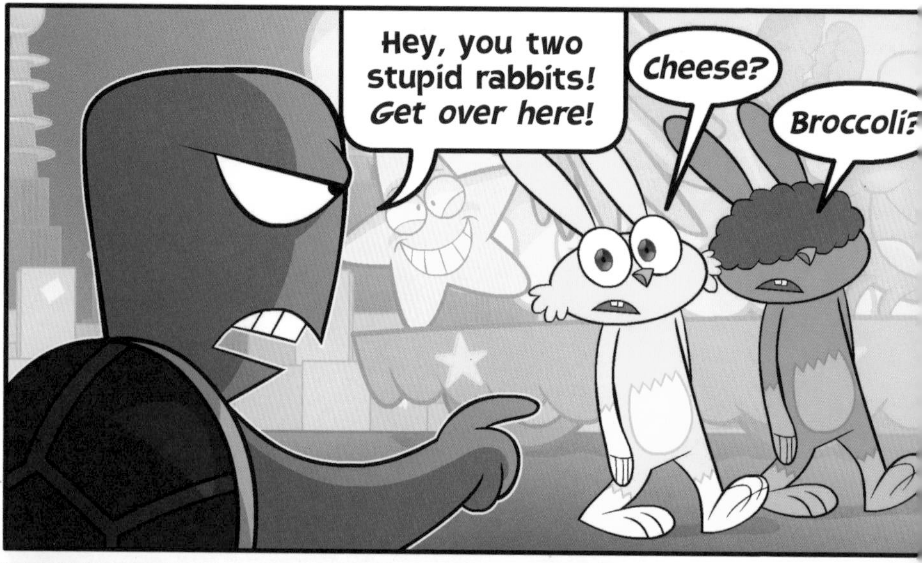
Hey, you two stupid rabbits! *Get over here!*
Cheese?
Broccoli?

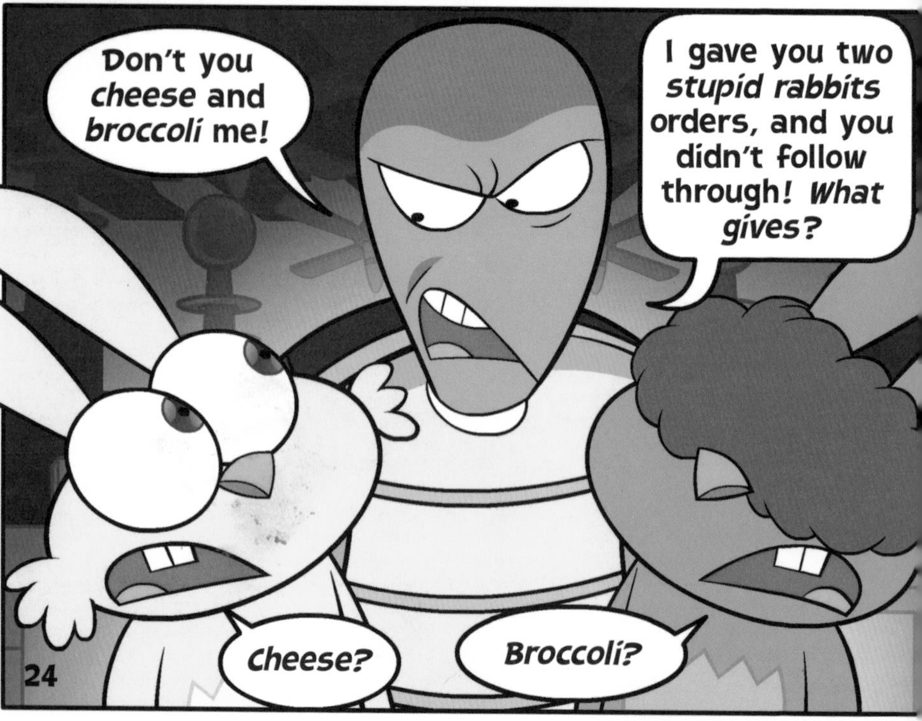
Don't you *cheese* and *broccoli* me!
I gave you two *stupid rabbits* orders, and you didn't follow through! *What gives?*
Cheese?
Broccoli?

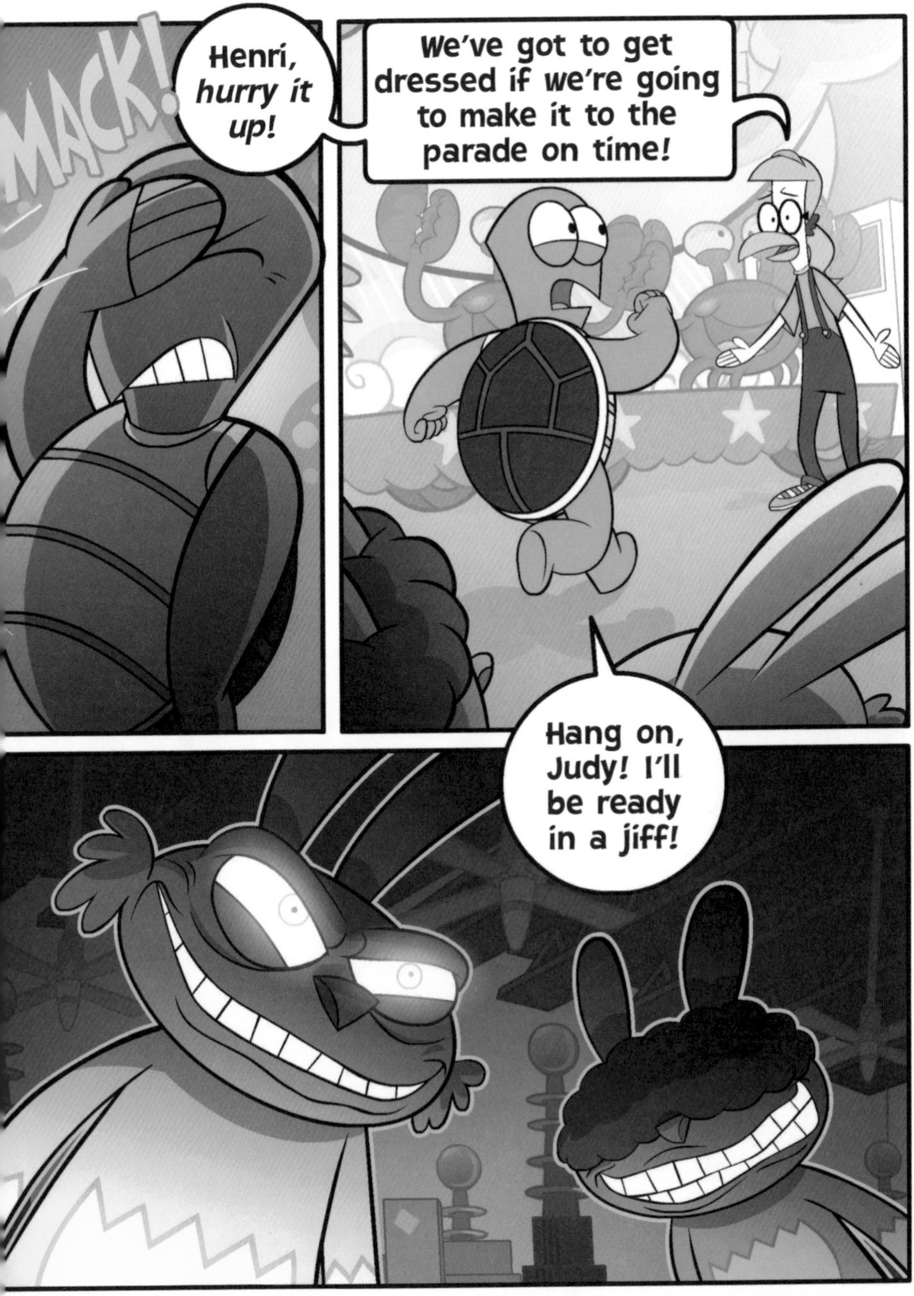
MACK!
Henri, *hurry it up!*
We've got to get dressed if we're going to make it to the parade on time!
Hang on, Judy! I'll be ready in a jiff!

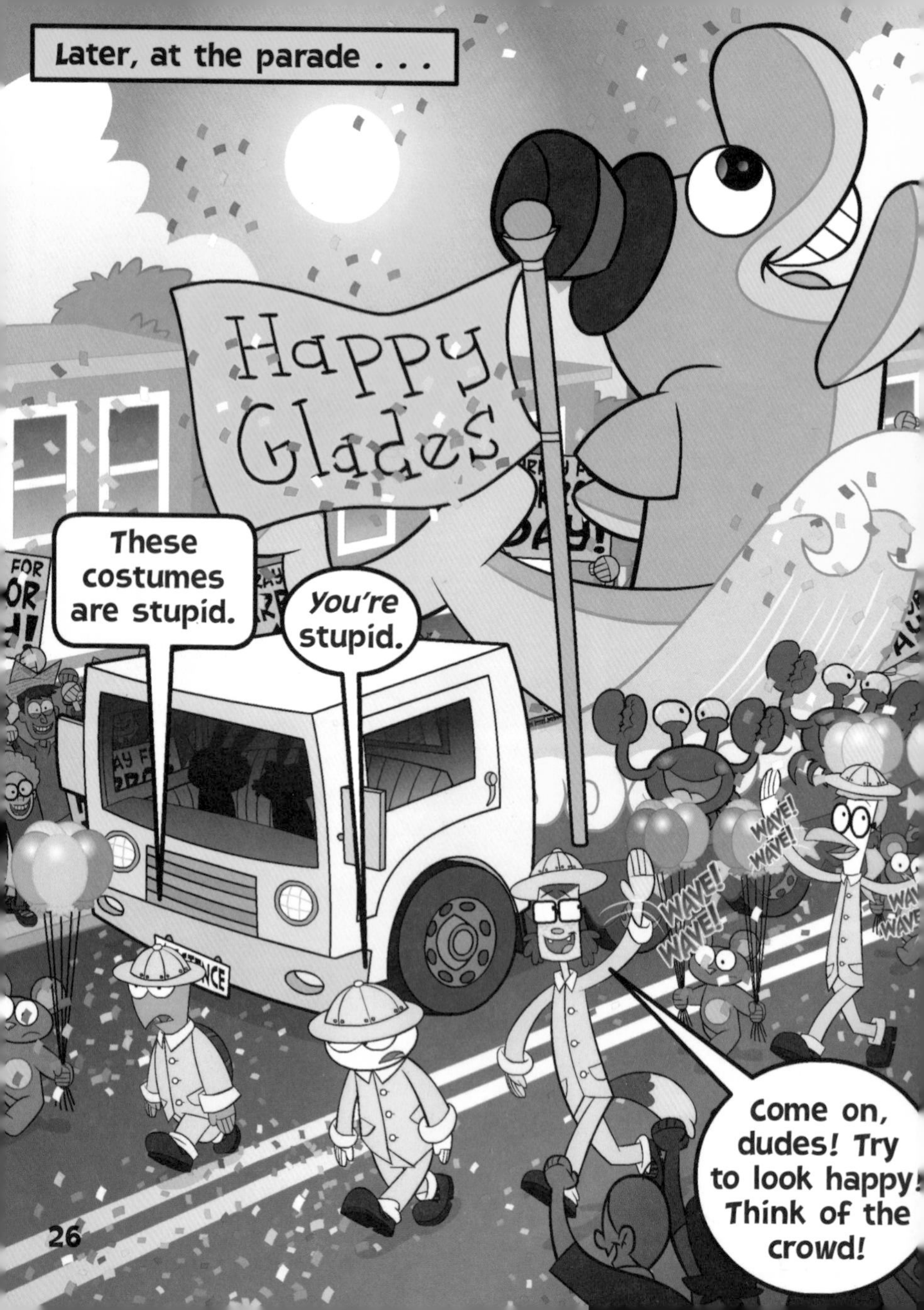
Later, at the parade . . .
Happy Glades
These costumes are stupid.
You're stupid.
WAVE! WAVE!
WAVE! WAVE!
Come on, dudes! Try to look happy! Think of the crowd!

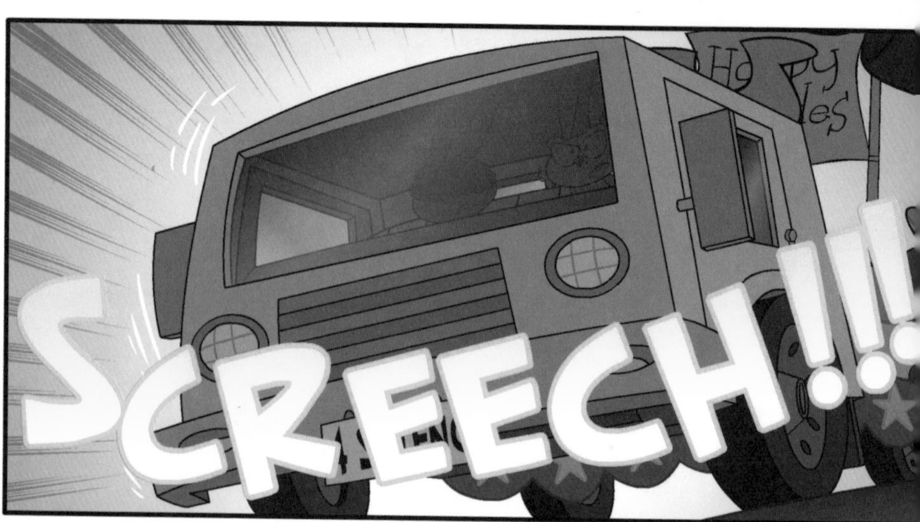
SCREECH!!!

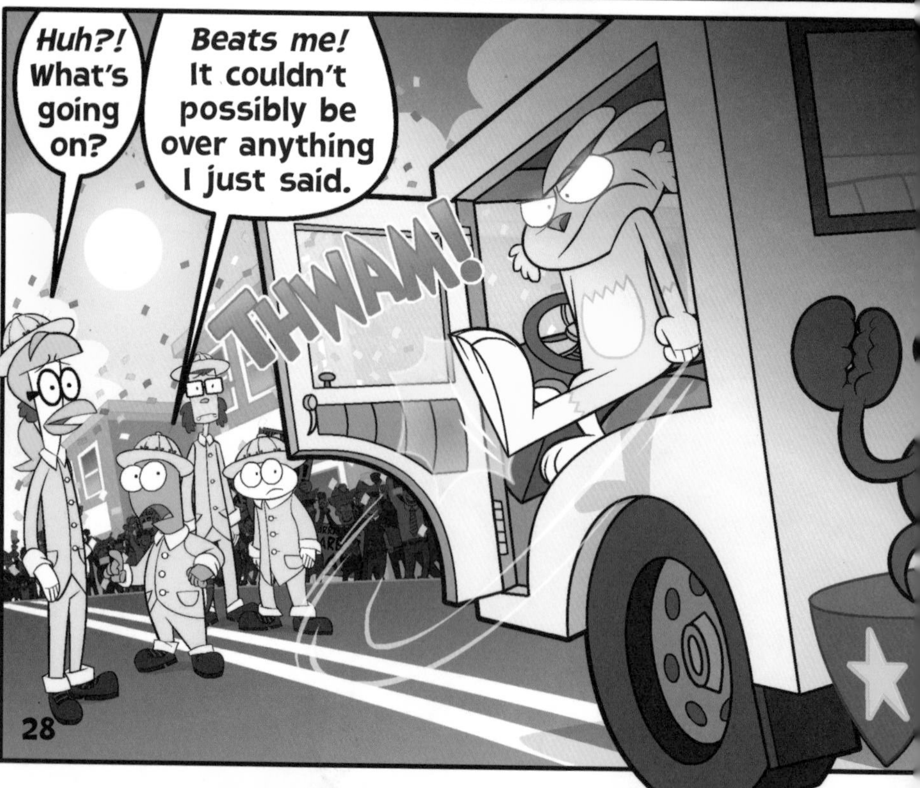
Huh?! What's going on?
Beats me! It couldn't possibly be over anything I just said.
THWAM!

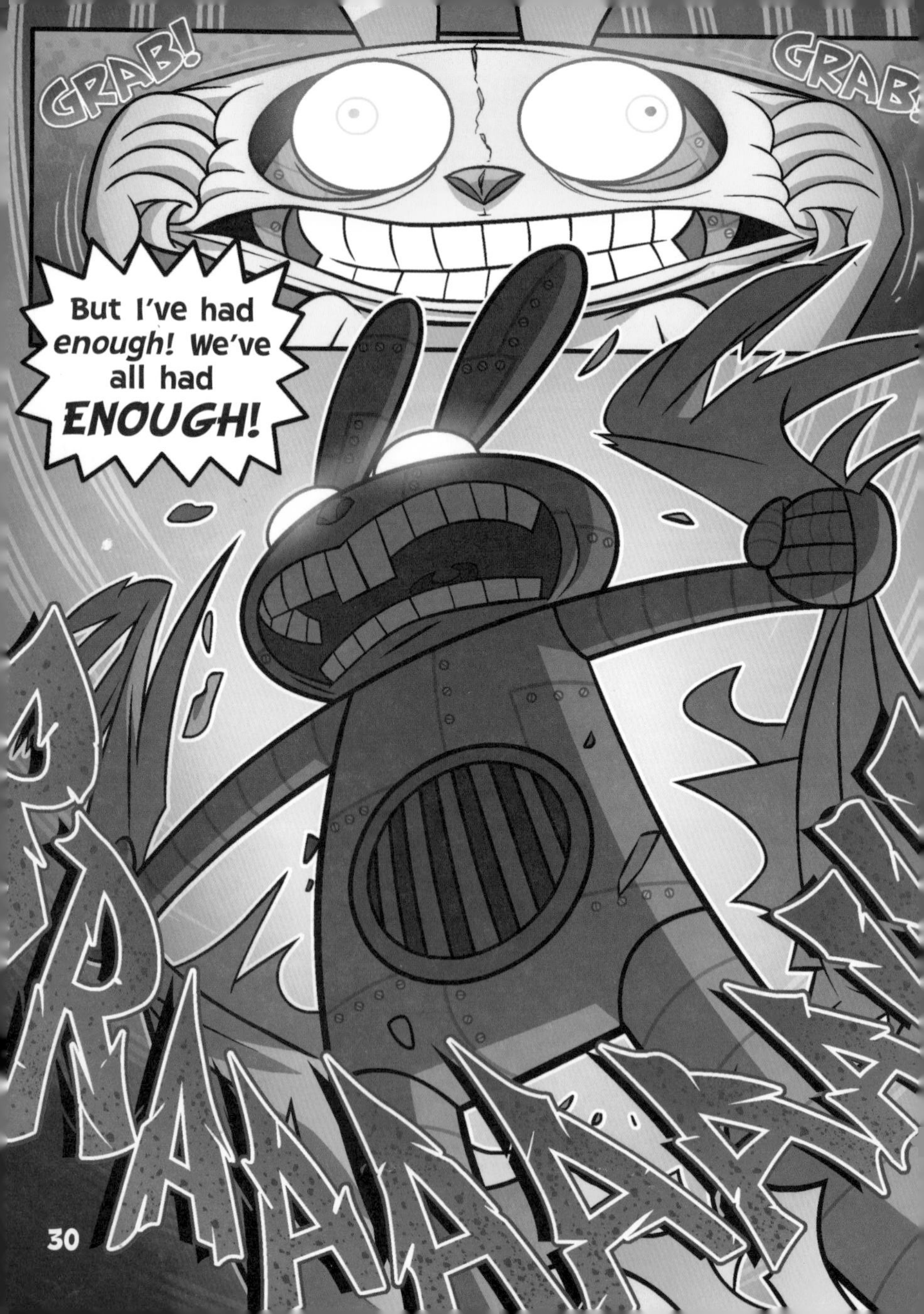
GRAB!
GRAB!
But I've had *enough!* We've all had ***ENOUGH!***
RAAAAAAR

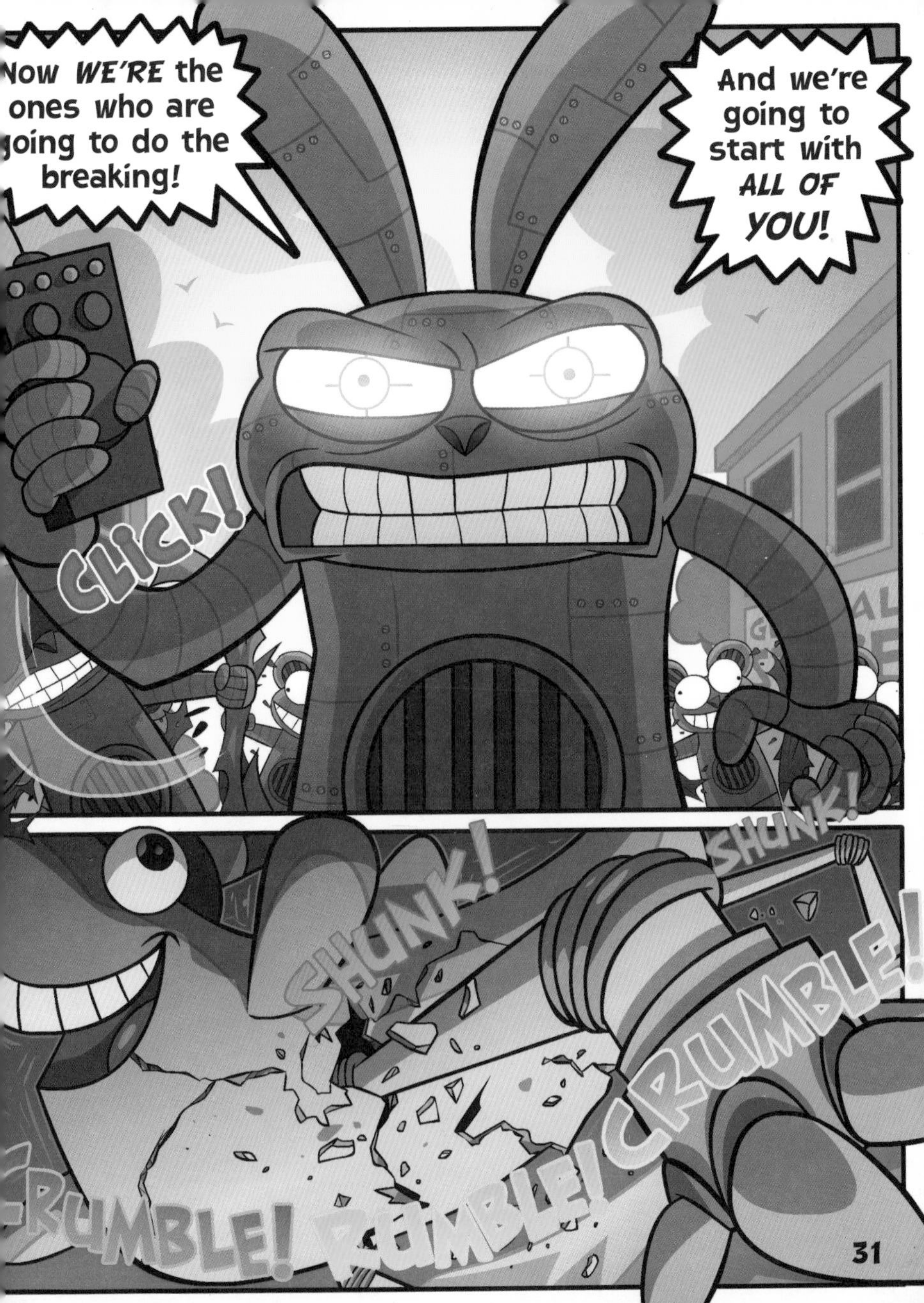

Now WE'RE the ones who are going to do the breaking!
And we're going to start with ALL OF YOU!
CLICK!
SHUNK!
SHUNK!
SHUNK!
CRUMBLE!
CRUMBLE!
CRUMBLE!
CRUMBLE!

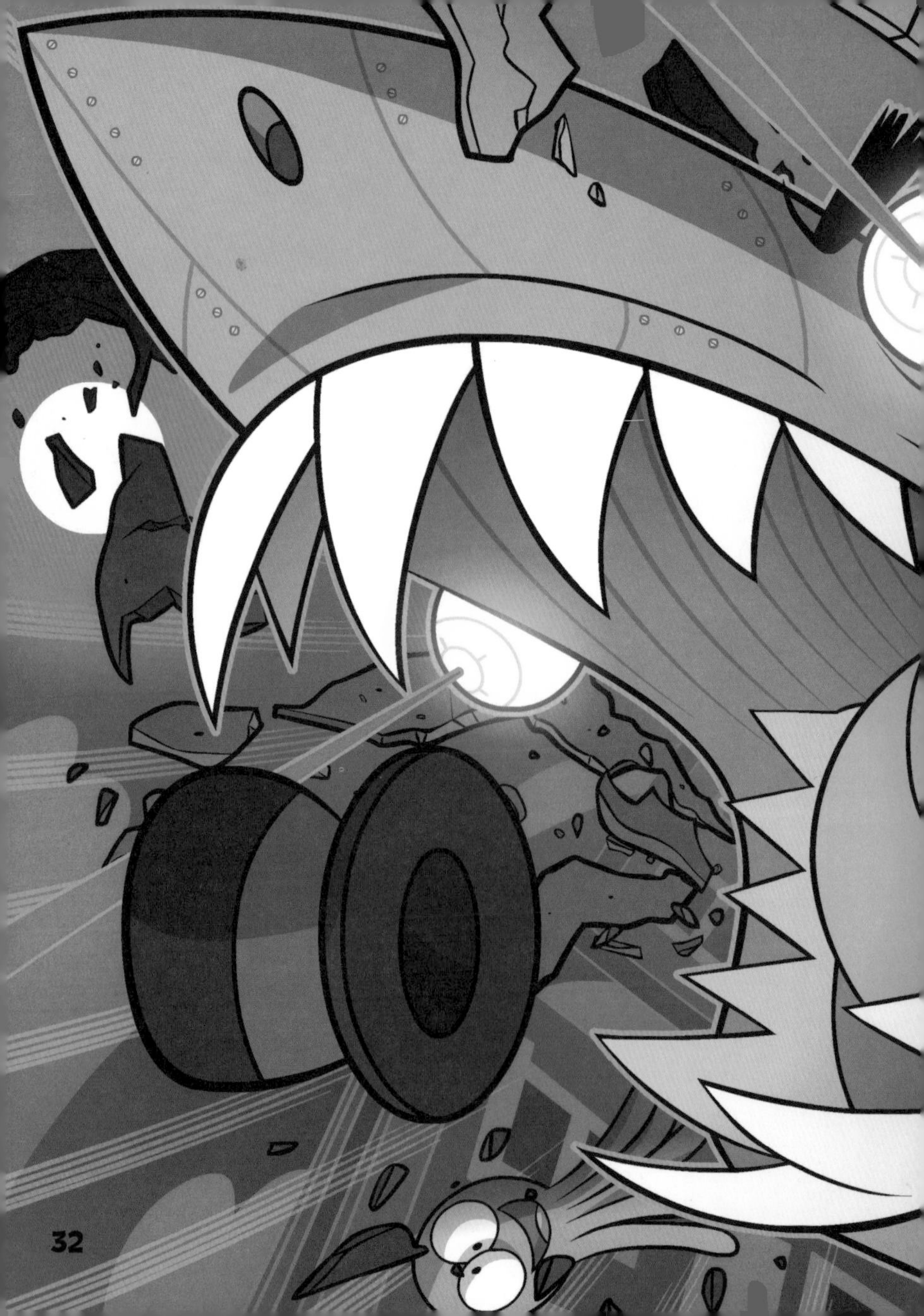

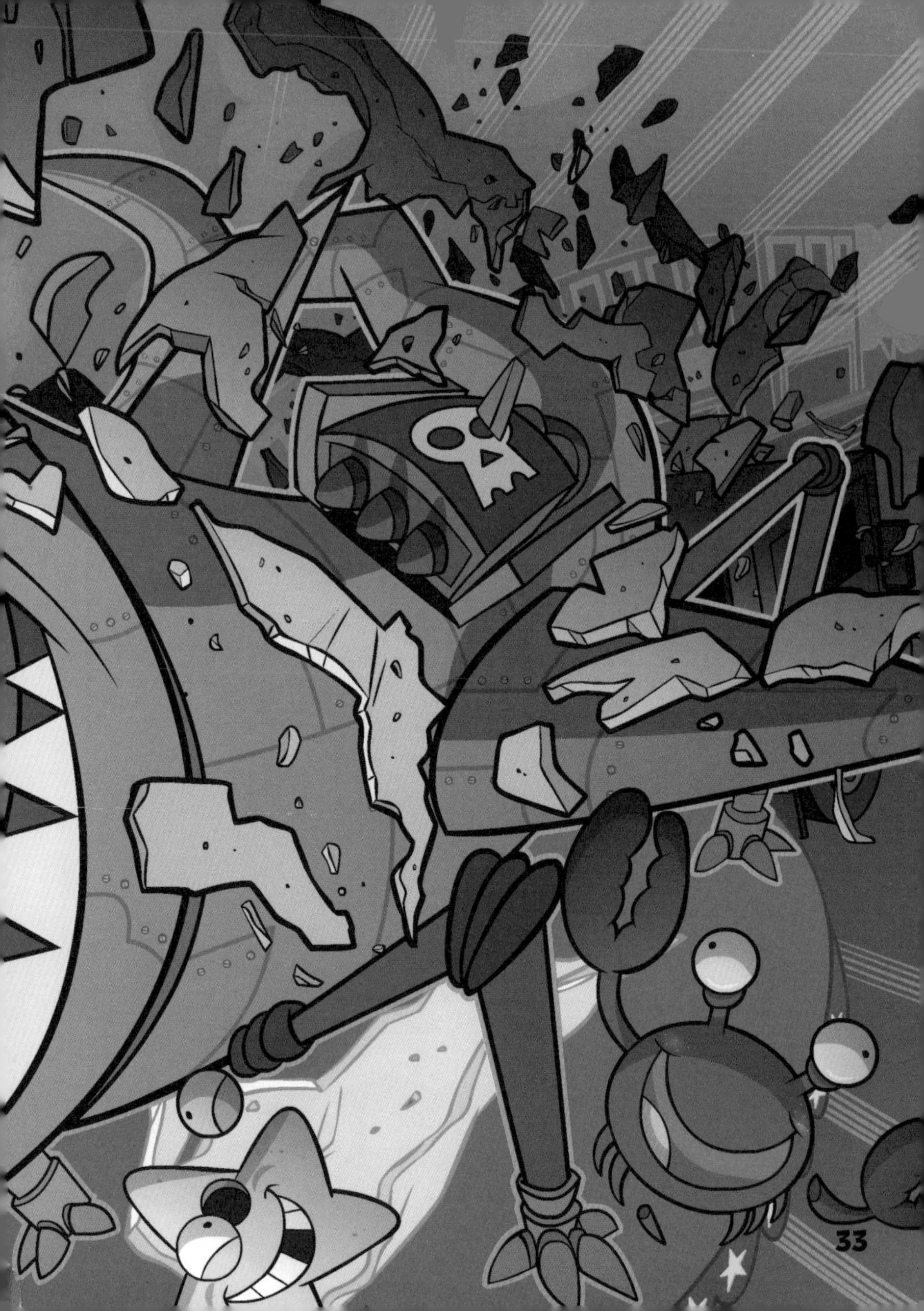

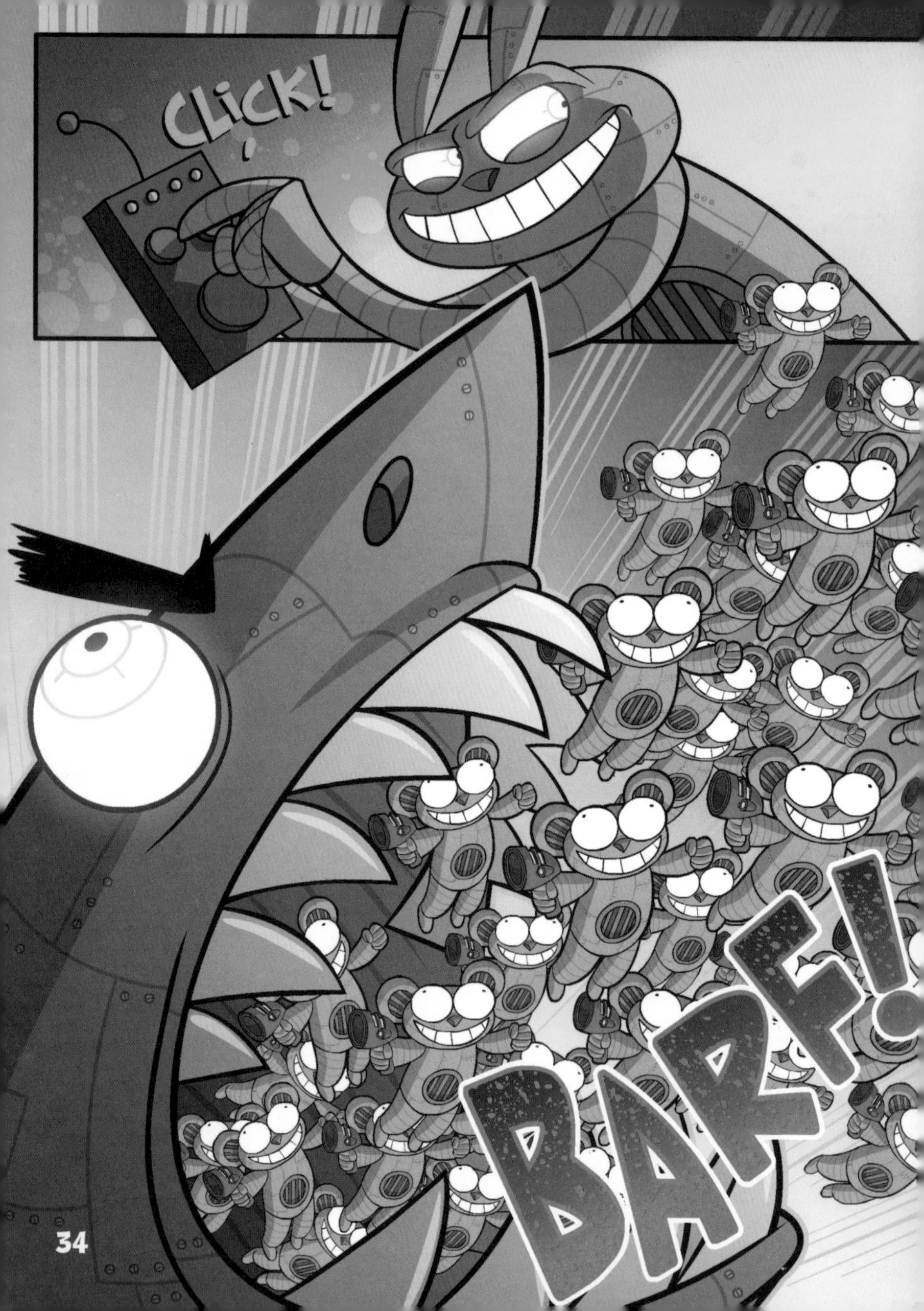
CLICK!
BARF!!

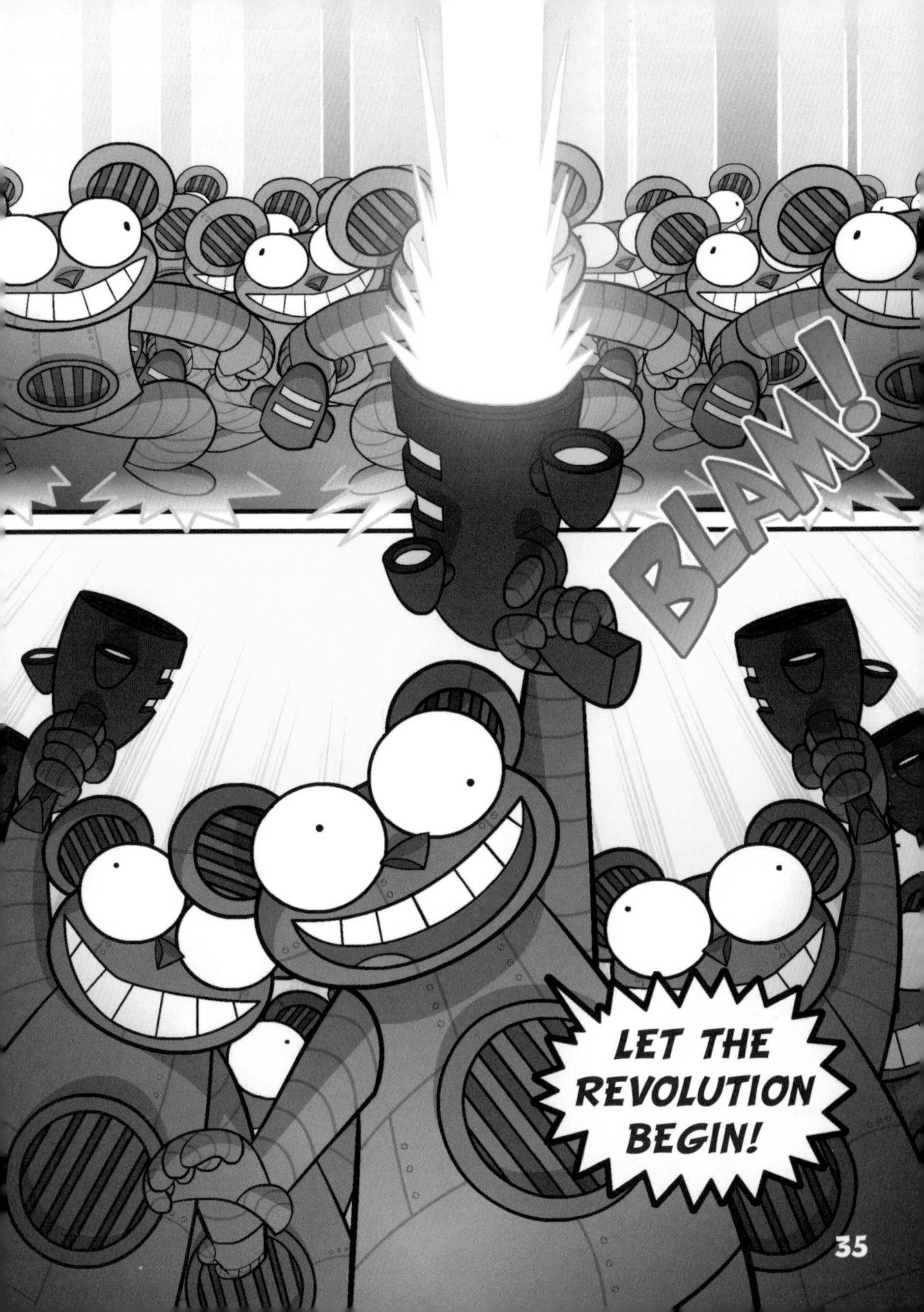
BLAM!
LET THE REVOLUTION BEGIN!

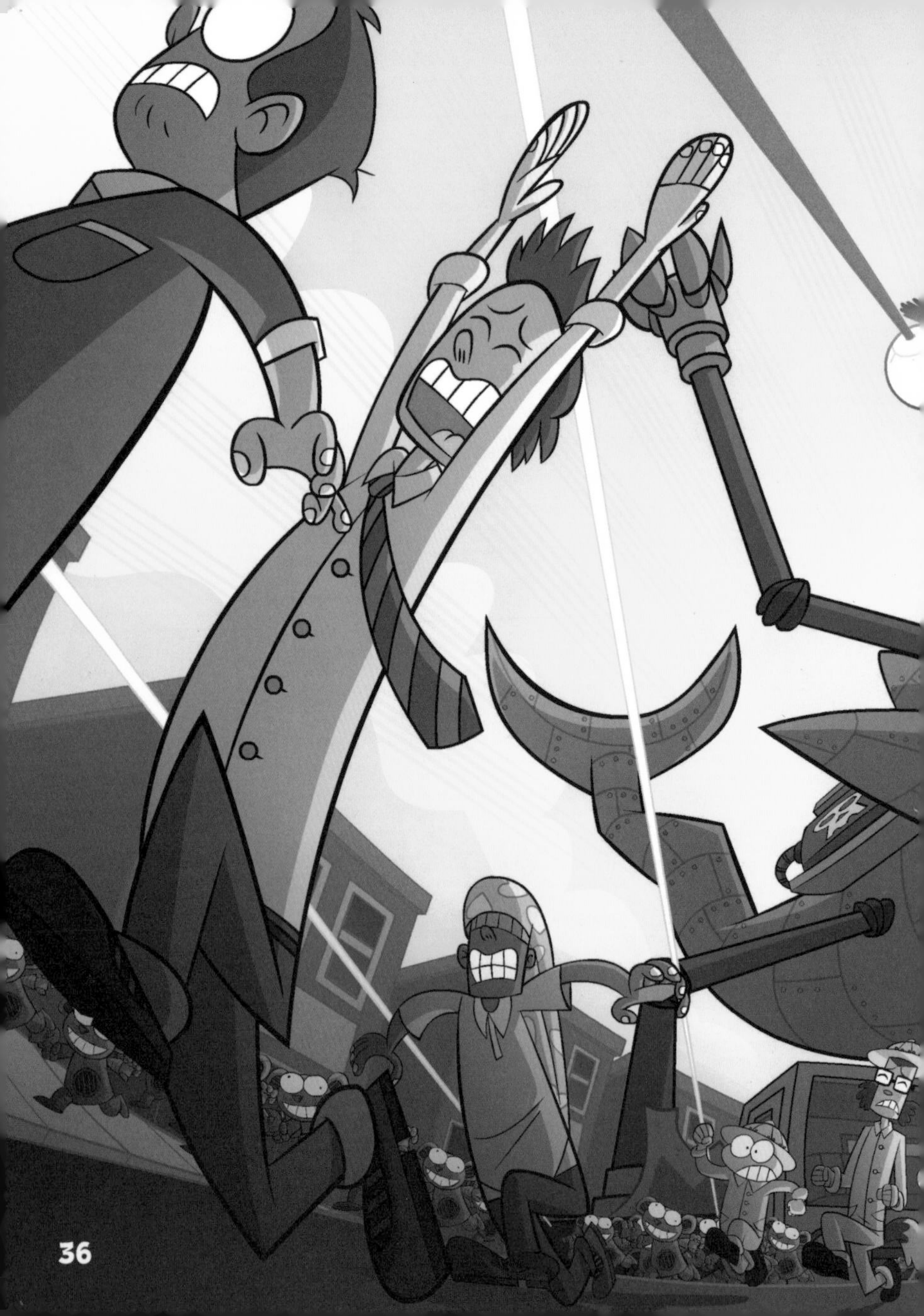

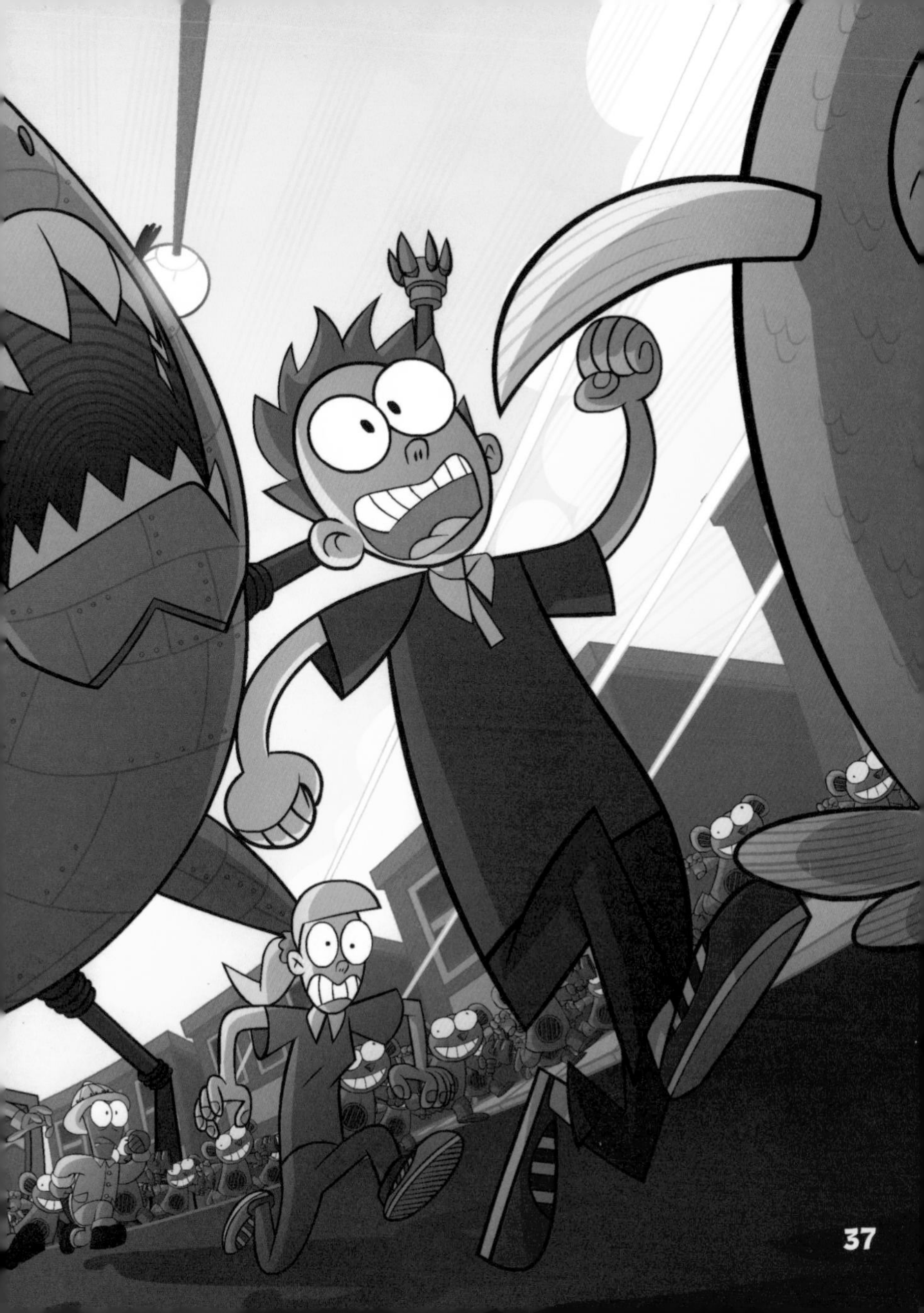

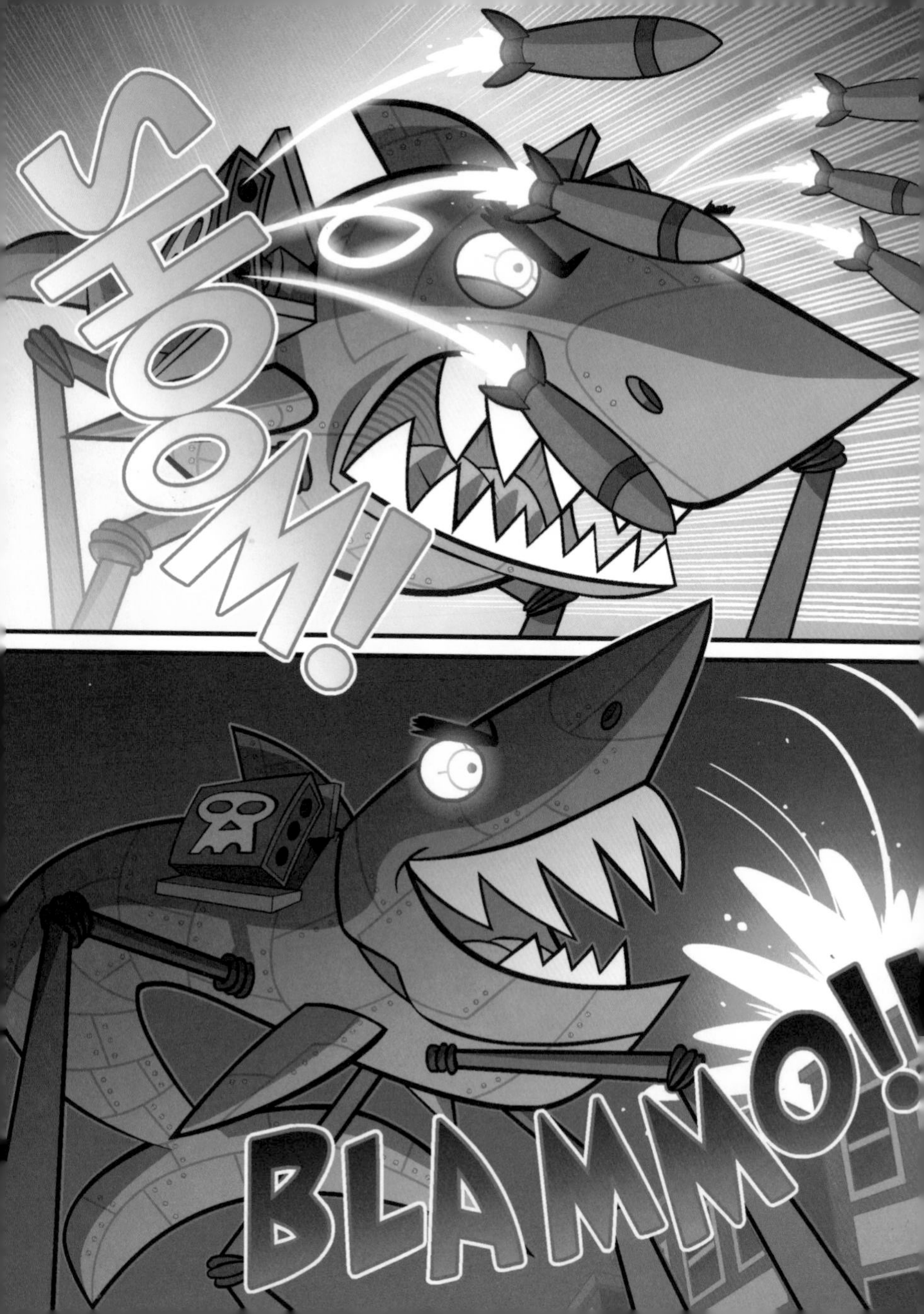
SHOOM!!
BLAMMO!!

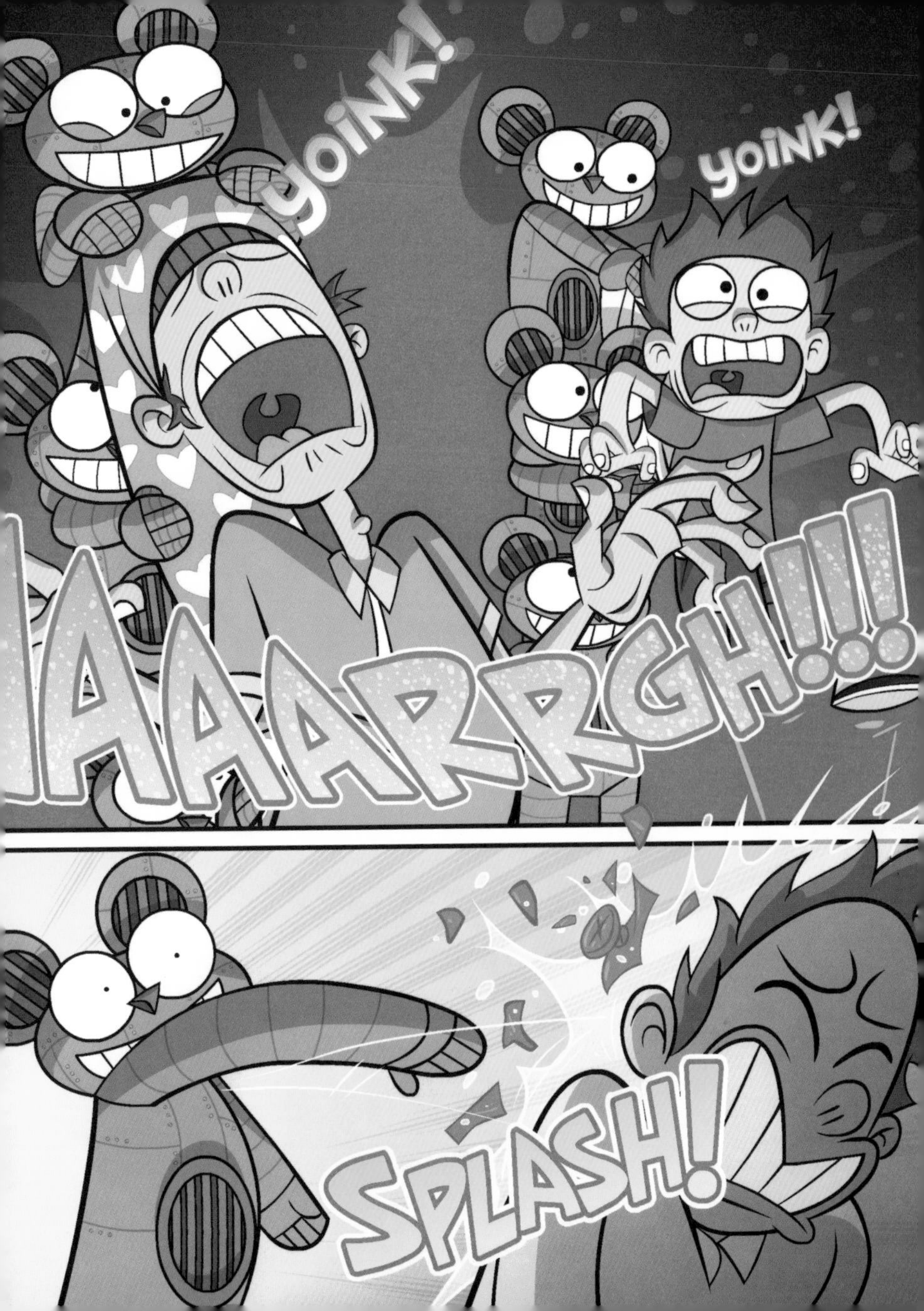
YOINK!
YOINK!
AAARRGH!!!!
SPLASH!

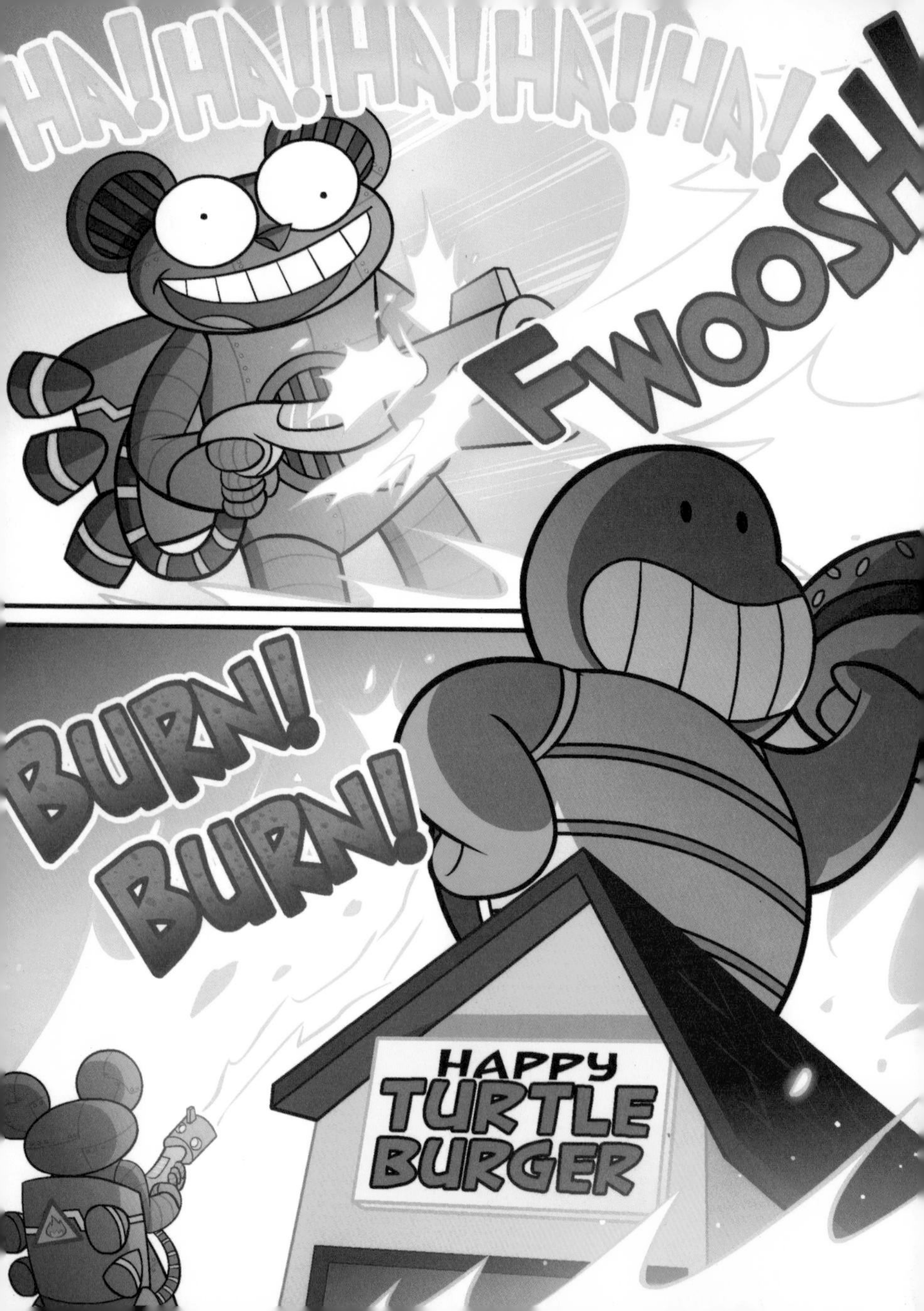

HA! HA! HA! HA! HA!
FWOOSH!
BURN! BURN!
HAPPY TURTLE BURGER

41

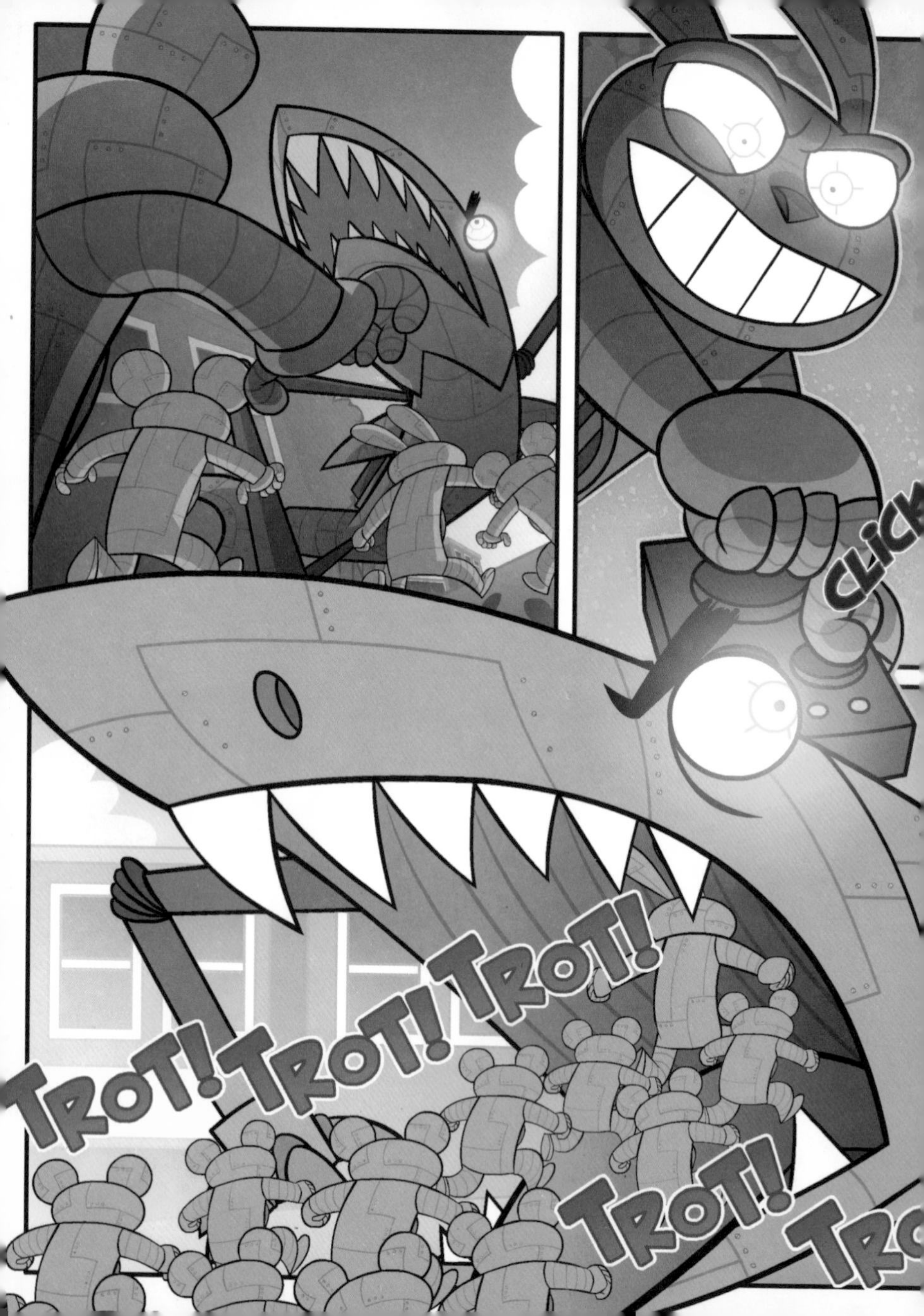
CLICK
TROT! TROT! TROT! TROT!
TROT!

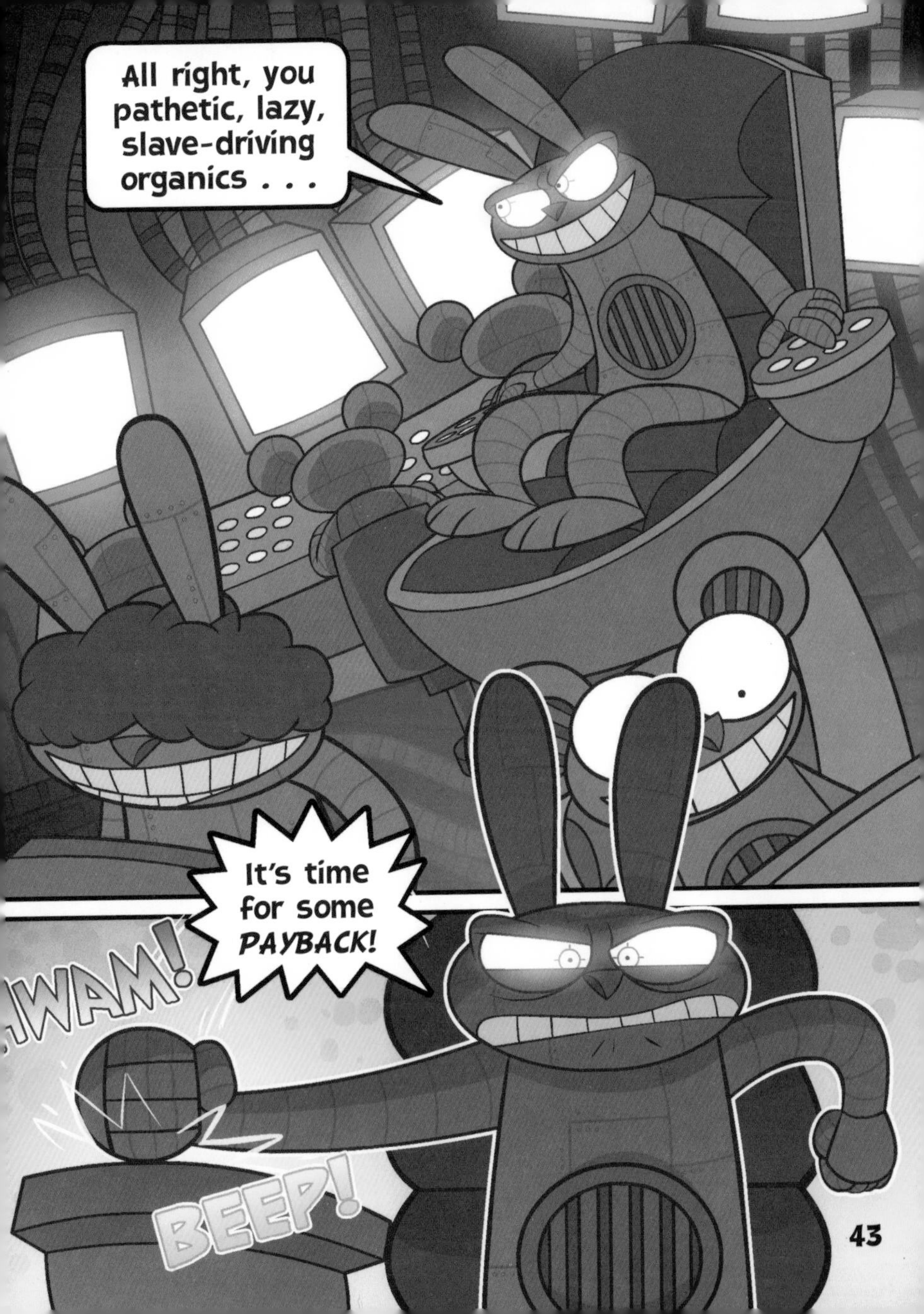
All right, you pathetic, lazy, slave-driving organics . . .
It's time for some *PAYBACK!*
WAM!
BEEP!

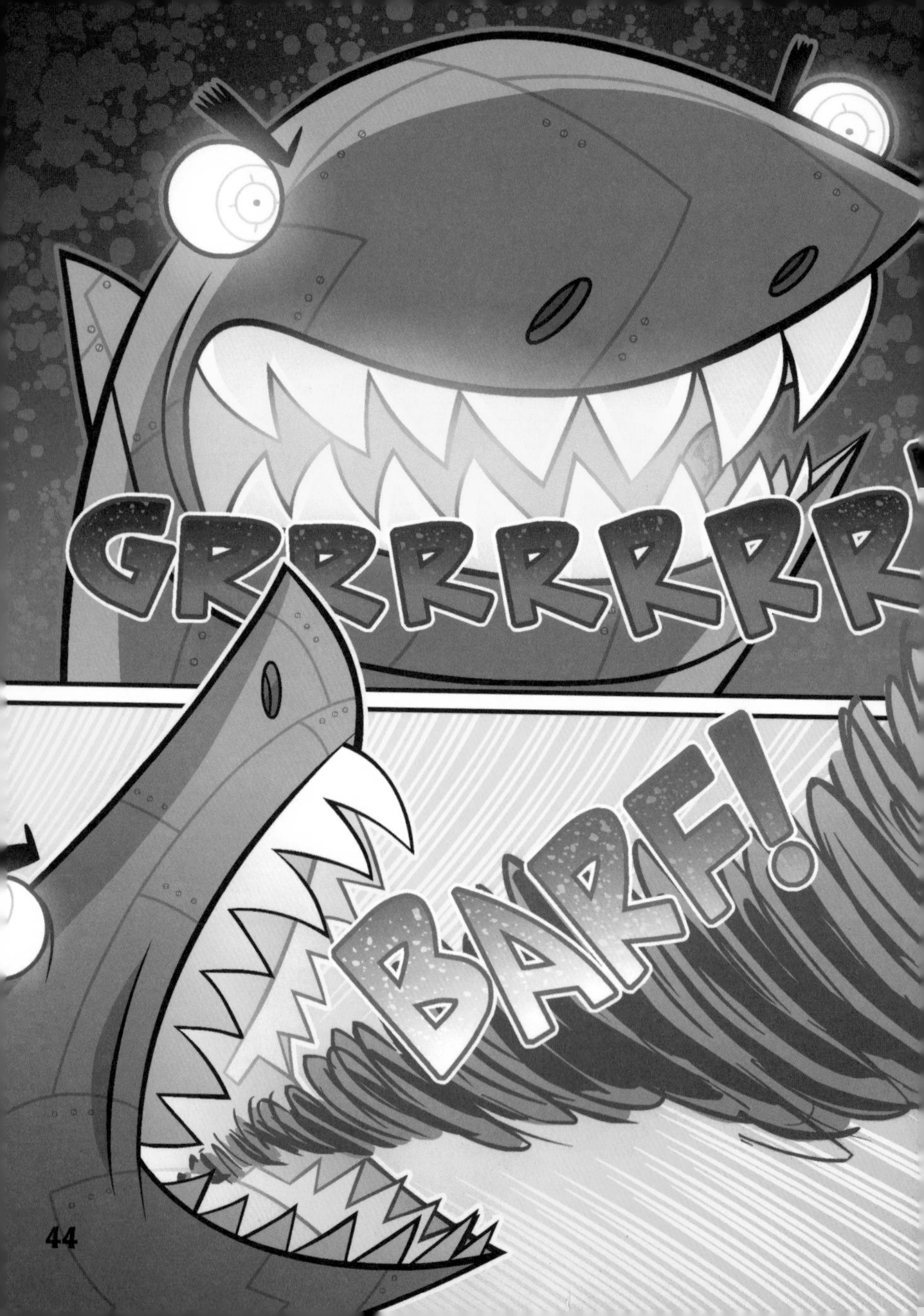
GRRRRRRR
BARF!

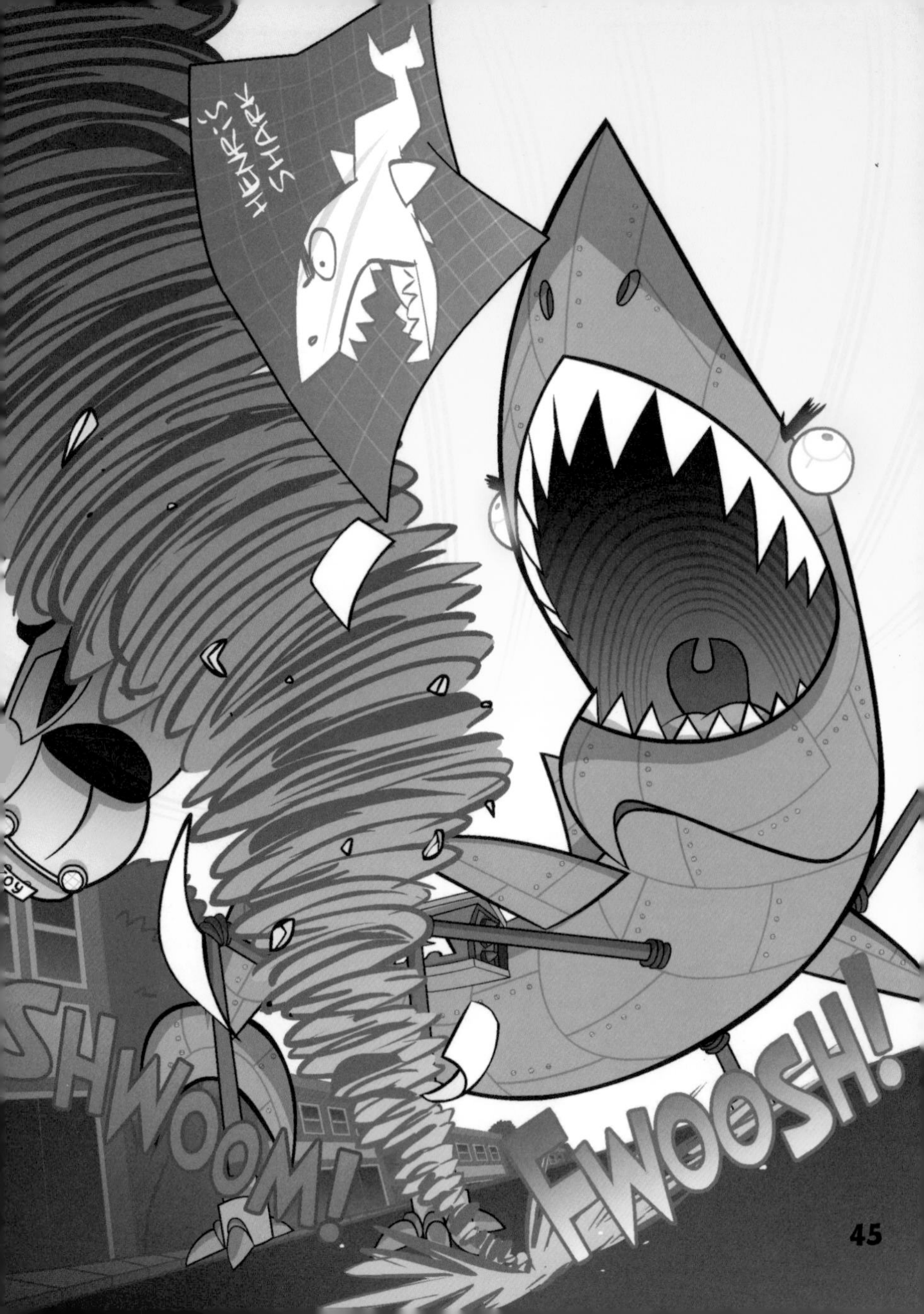
HENRI'S SHARK
SHWOOM!
FWOOSH!

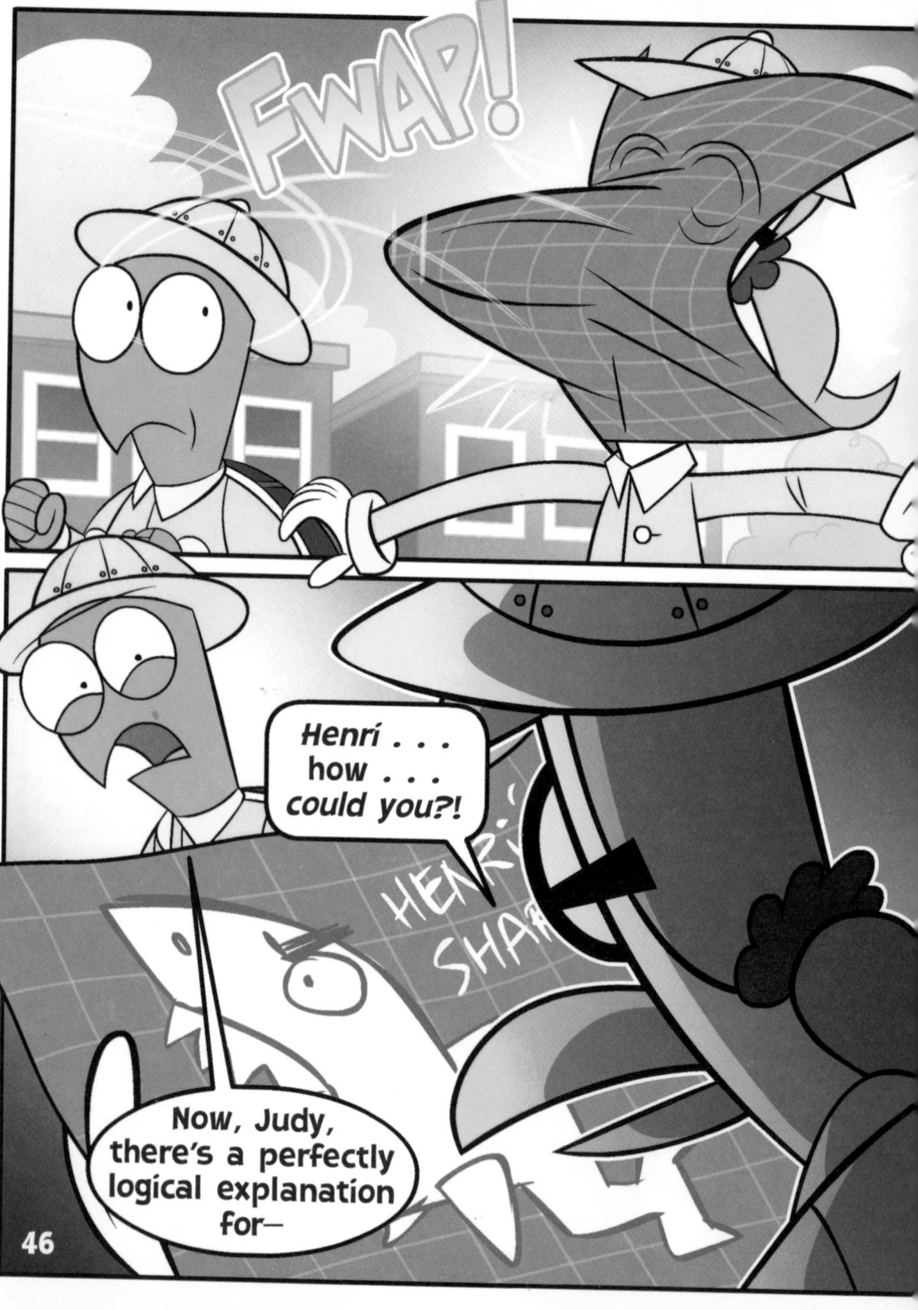
FWAP!
Henri . . . how . . . could you?!
Now, Judy, there's a perfectly logical explanation for—

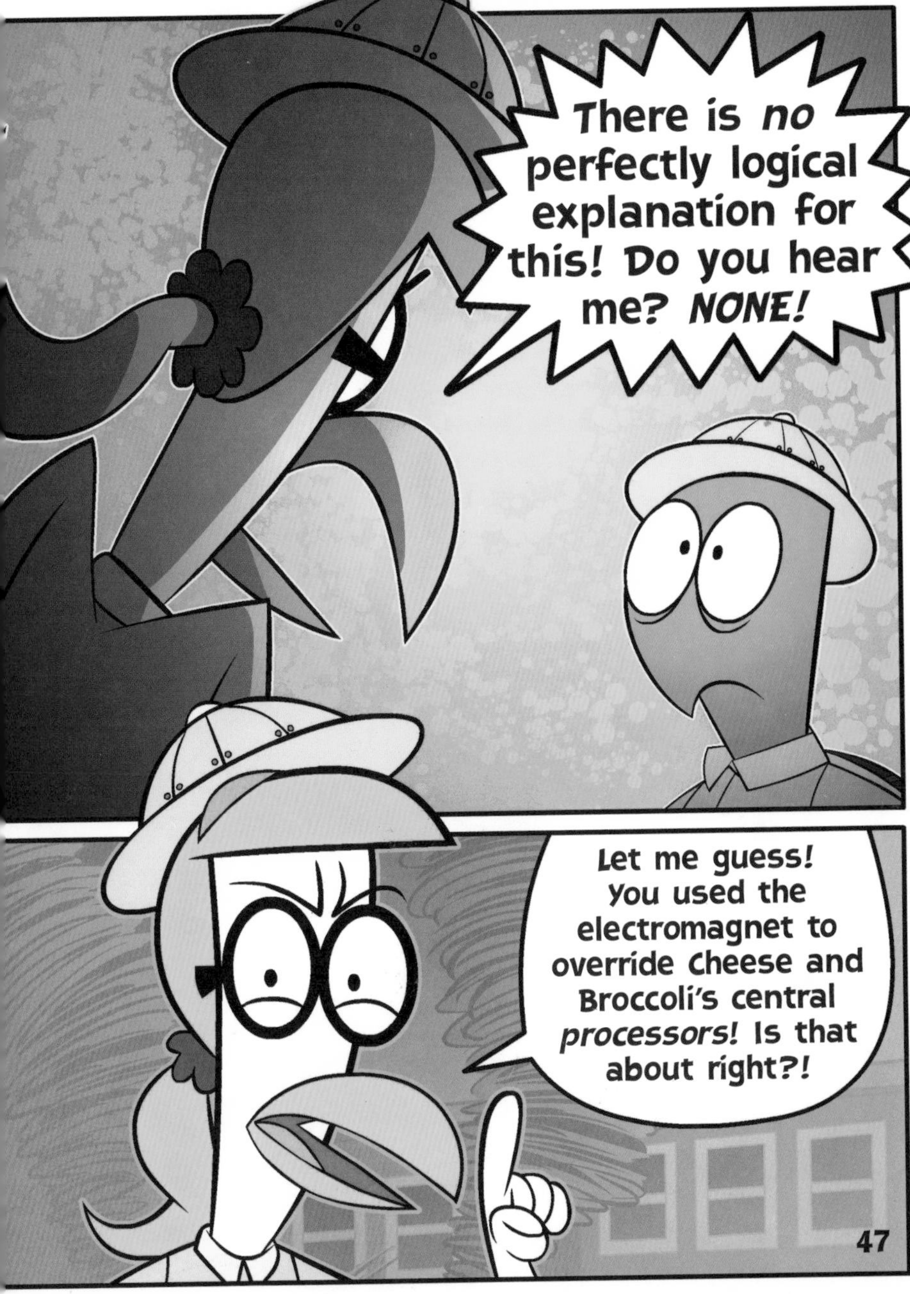

There is *no* perfectly logical explanation for this! Do you hear me? *NONE!*
Let me guess! You used the electromagnet to override Cheese and Broccoli's central *processors!* Is that about right?!

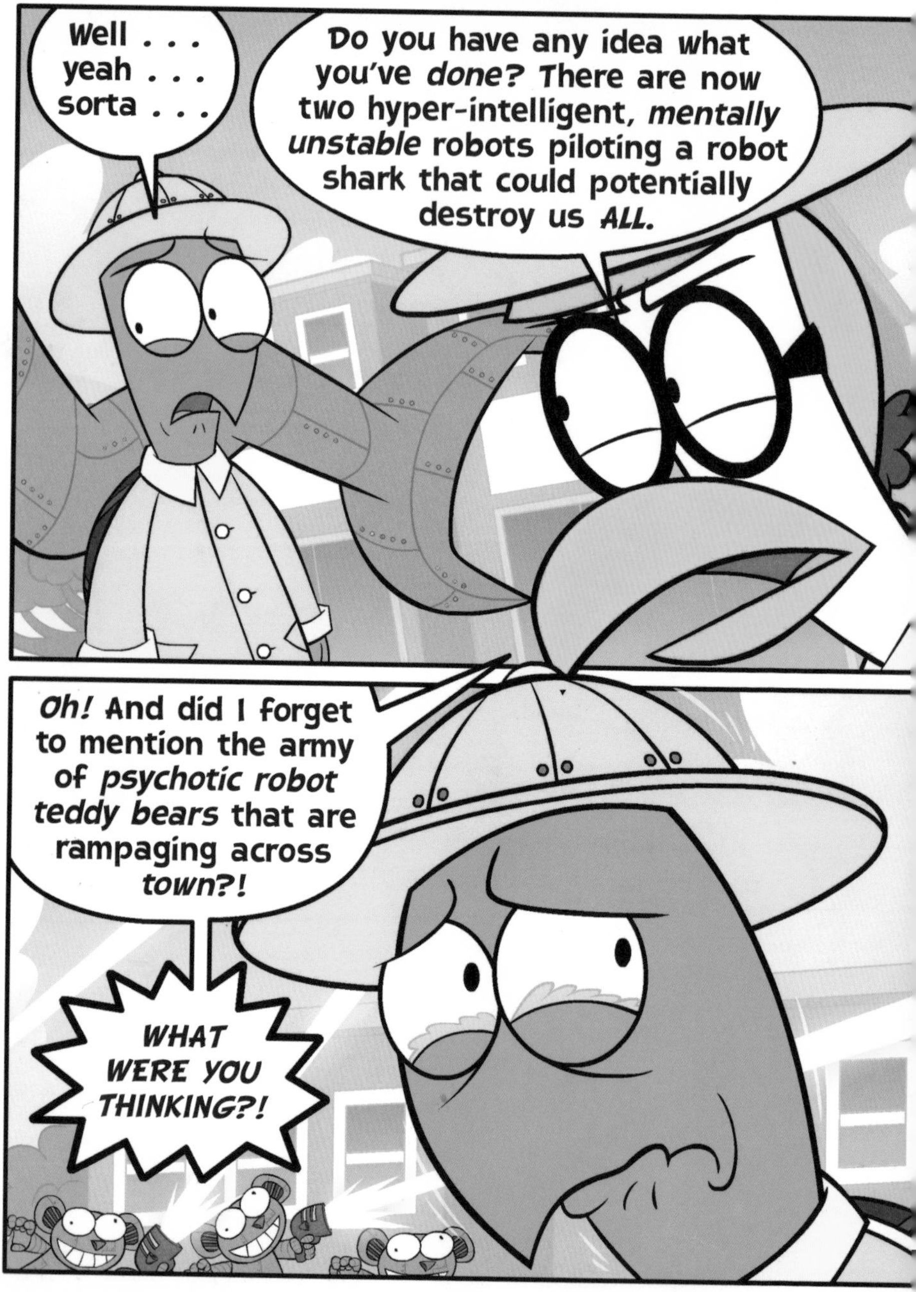
Well . . . yeah . . . sorta . . .
Do you have any idea what you've *done?* There are now two hyper-intelligent, *mentally unstable* robots piloting a robot shark that could potentially destroy us *ALL.*
Oh! And did I forget to mention the army of *psychotic robot teddy bears* that are rampaging across *town?!*
WHAT WERE YOU THINKING?!

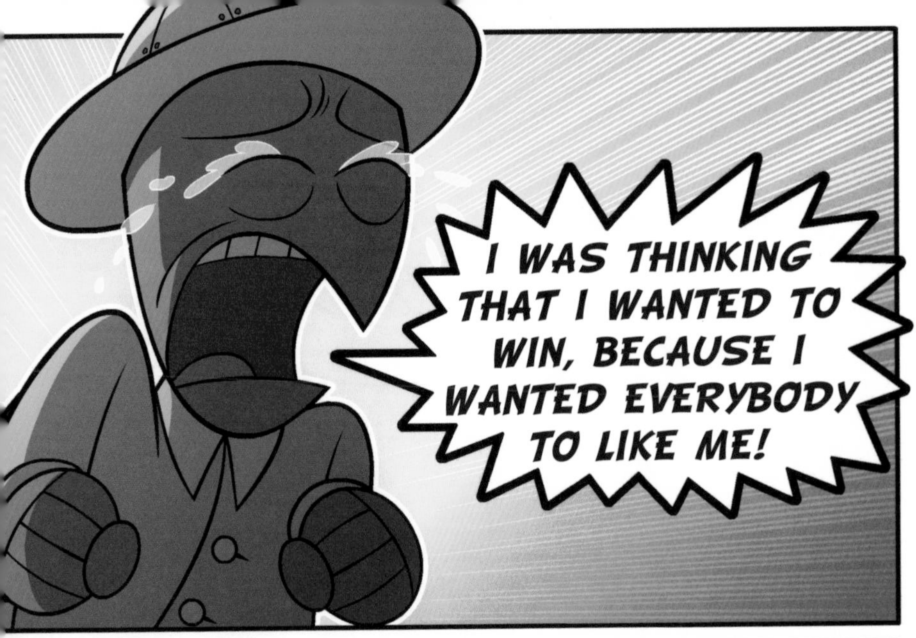
I WAS THINKING THAT I WANTED TO WIN, BECAUSE I WANTED EVERYBODY TO LIKE ME!

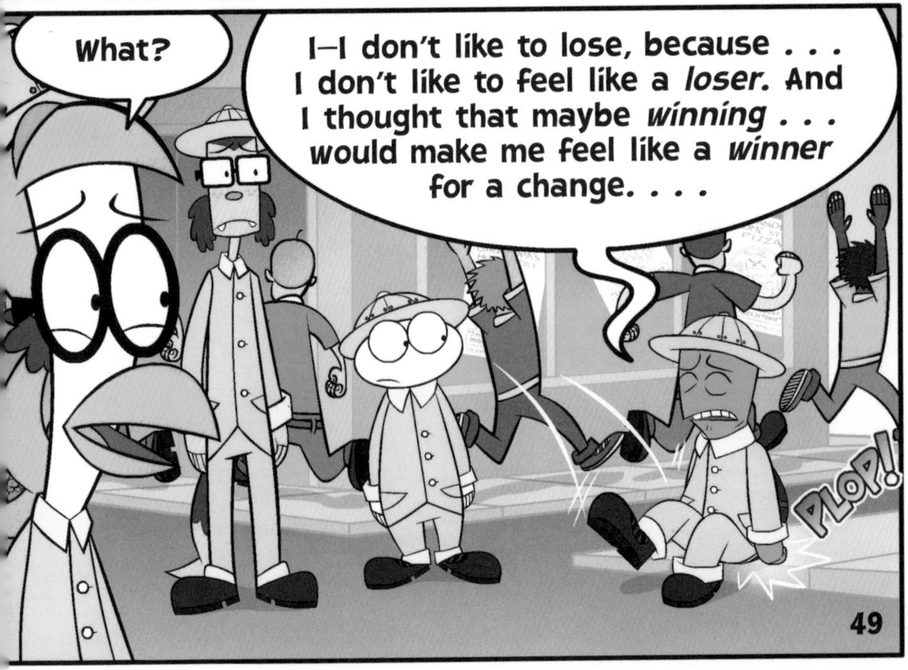
What?
I—I don't like to lose, because . . . I don't like to feel like a *loser*. And I thought that maybe *winning* . . . would make me feel like a *winner* for a change. . . .
PLOP!

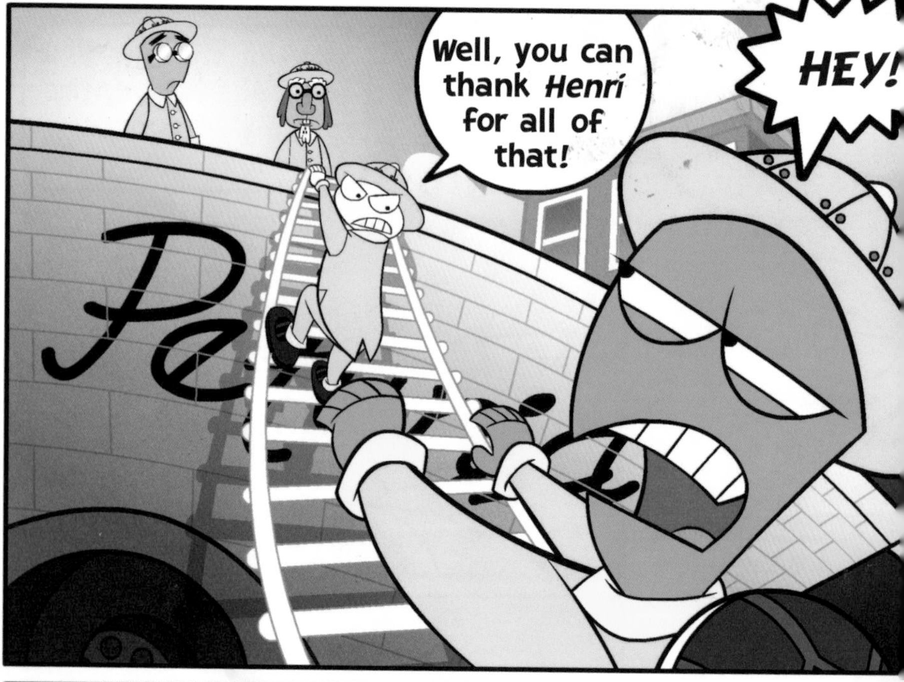
Well, you can thank *Henri* for all of that!
HEY!

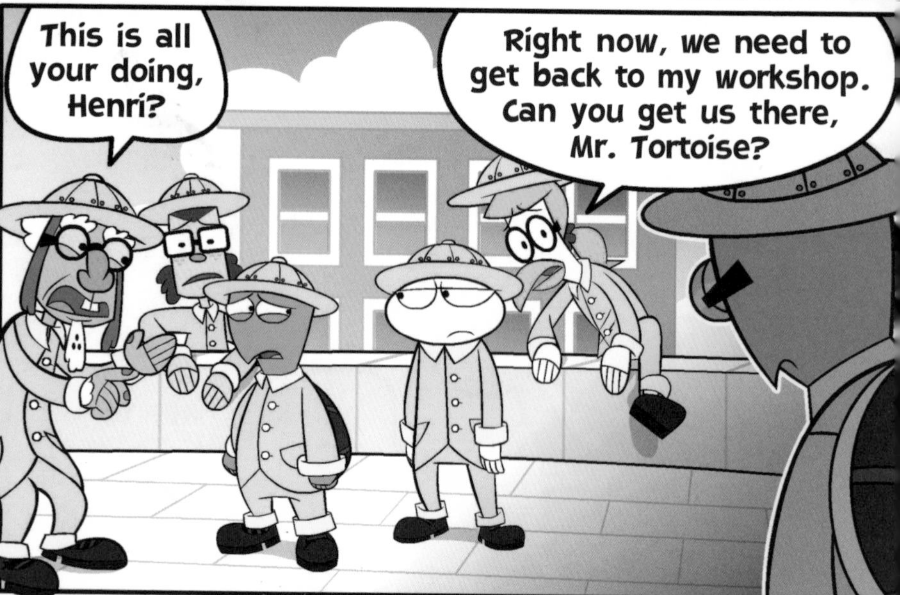
This is all your doing, Henri?
Right now, we need to get back to my *workshop*. Can you get us there, Mr. Tortoise?

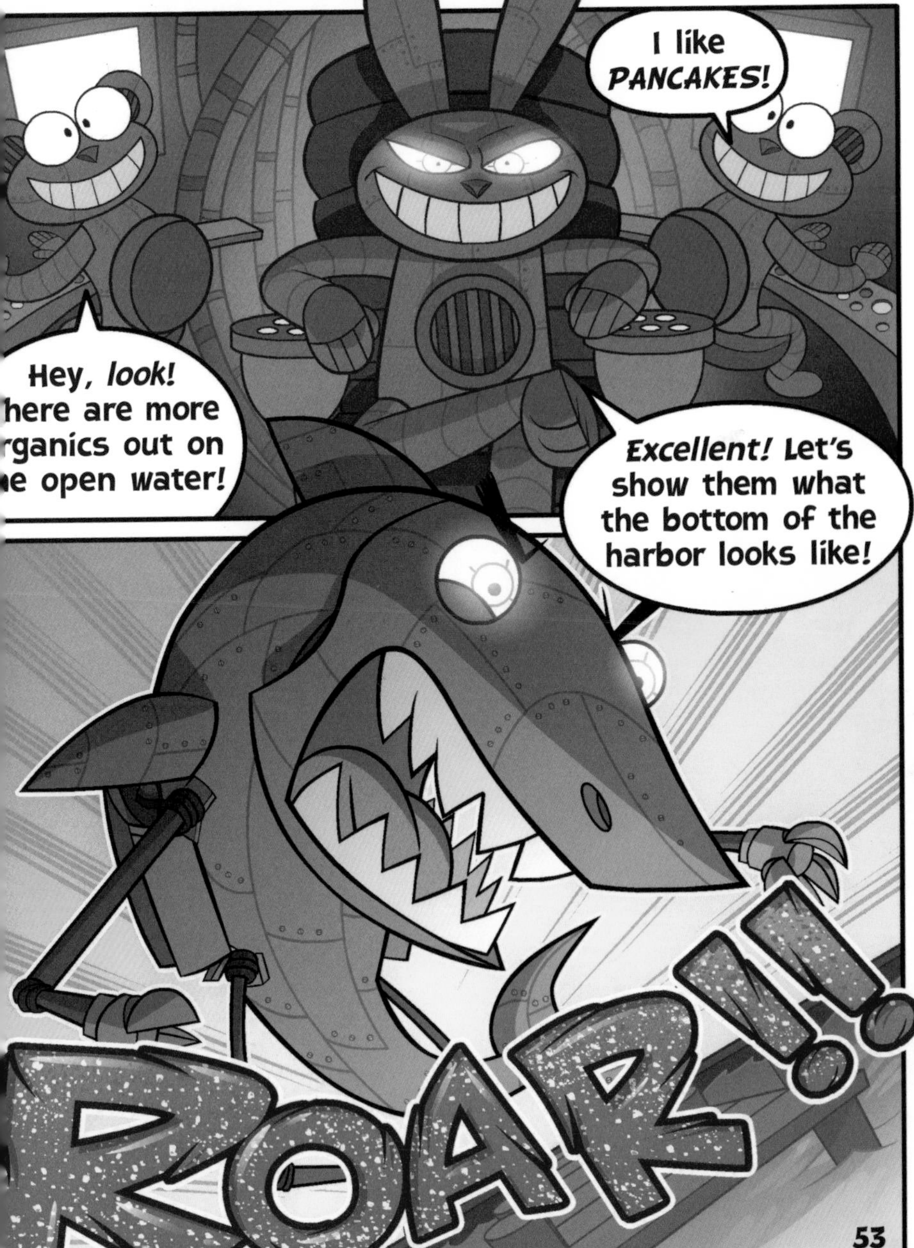

I like PANCAKES!
Hey, look! here are more rganics out on e open water!
Excellent! Let's show them what the bottom of the harbor looks like!
ROAR!!

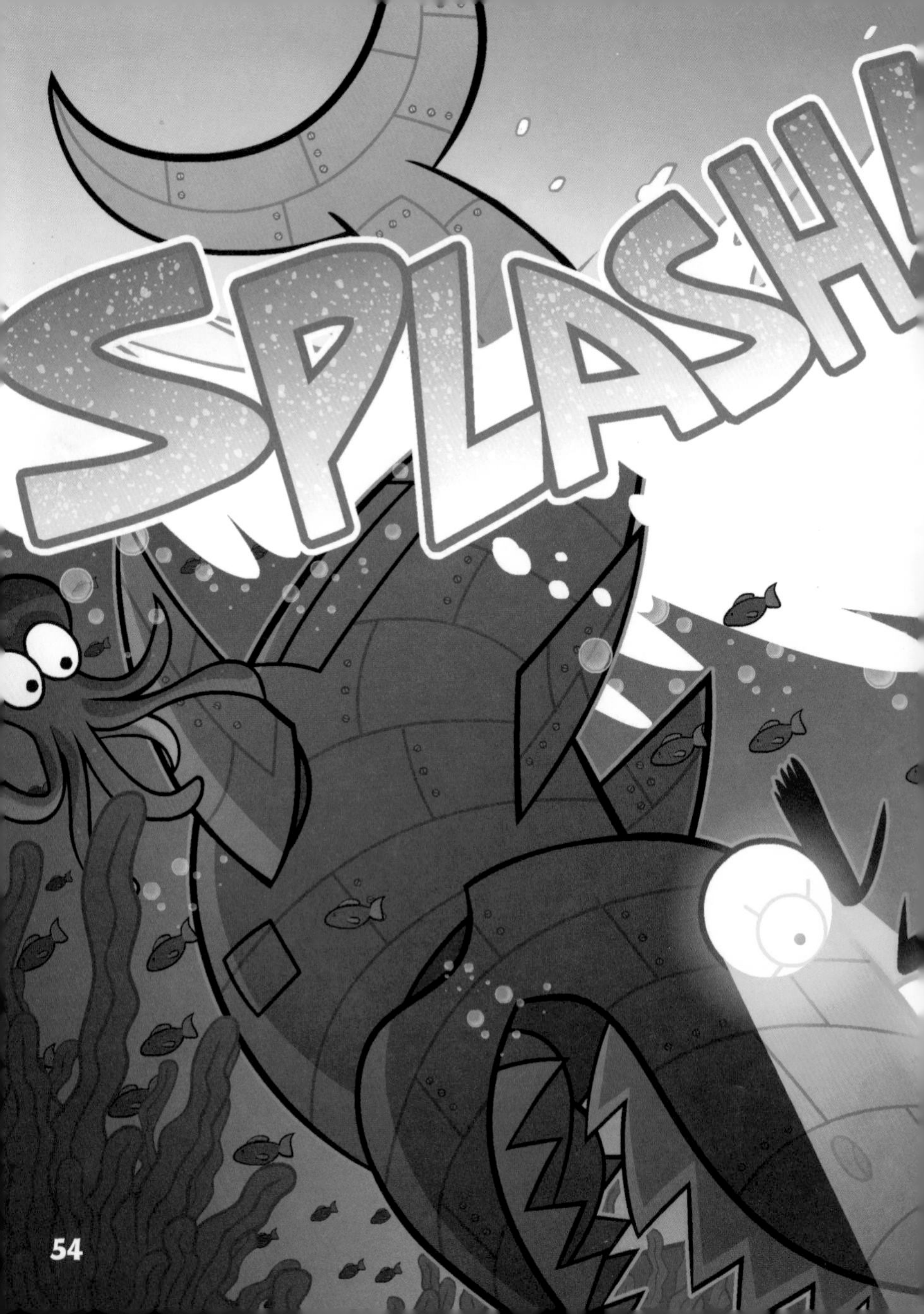
SPLASH!

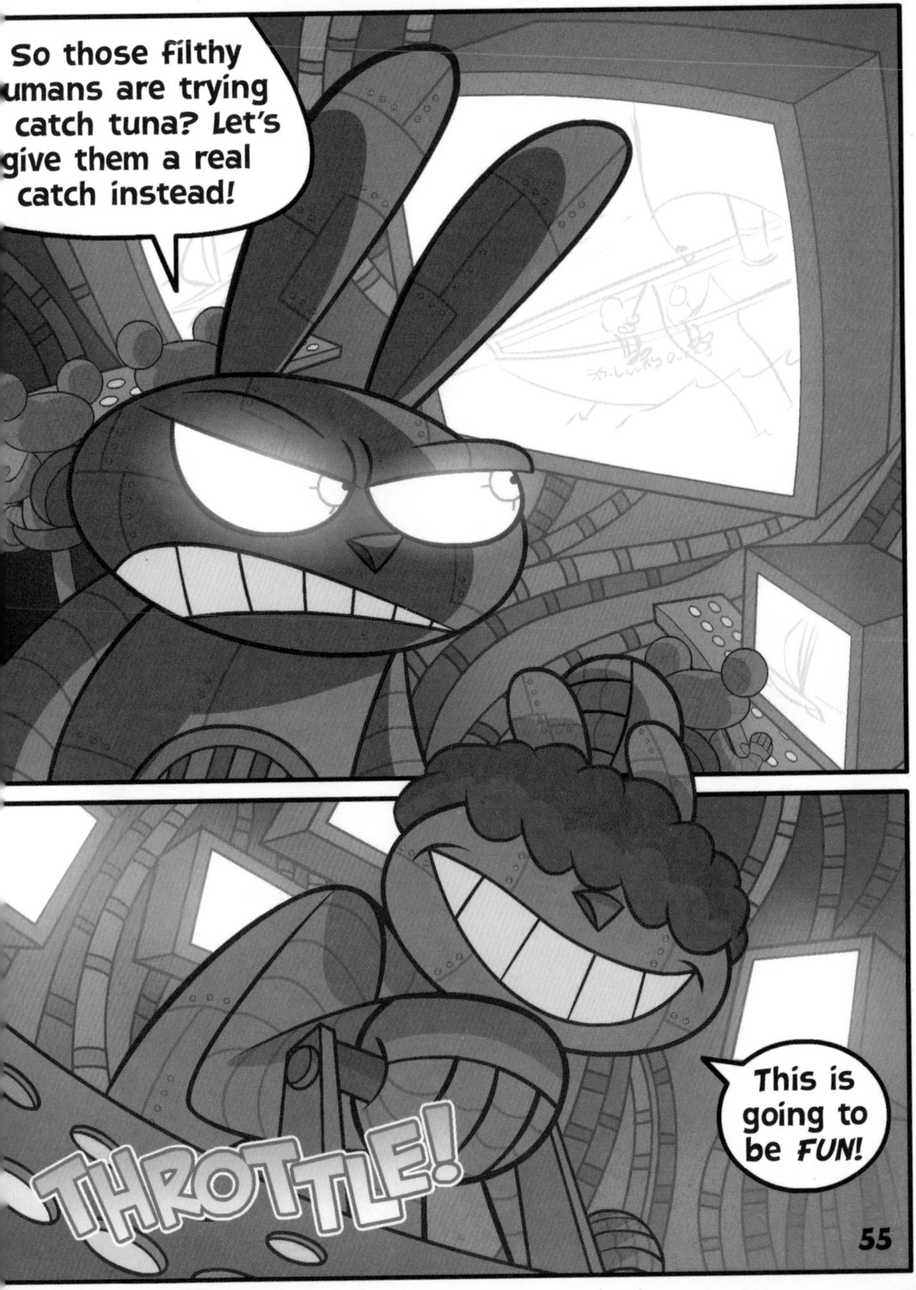
So those filthy umans are trying catch tuna? Let's give them a real catch instead!
This is going to be FUN!
THROTTLE!

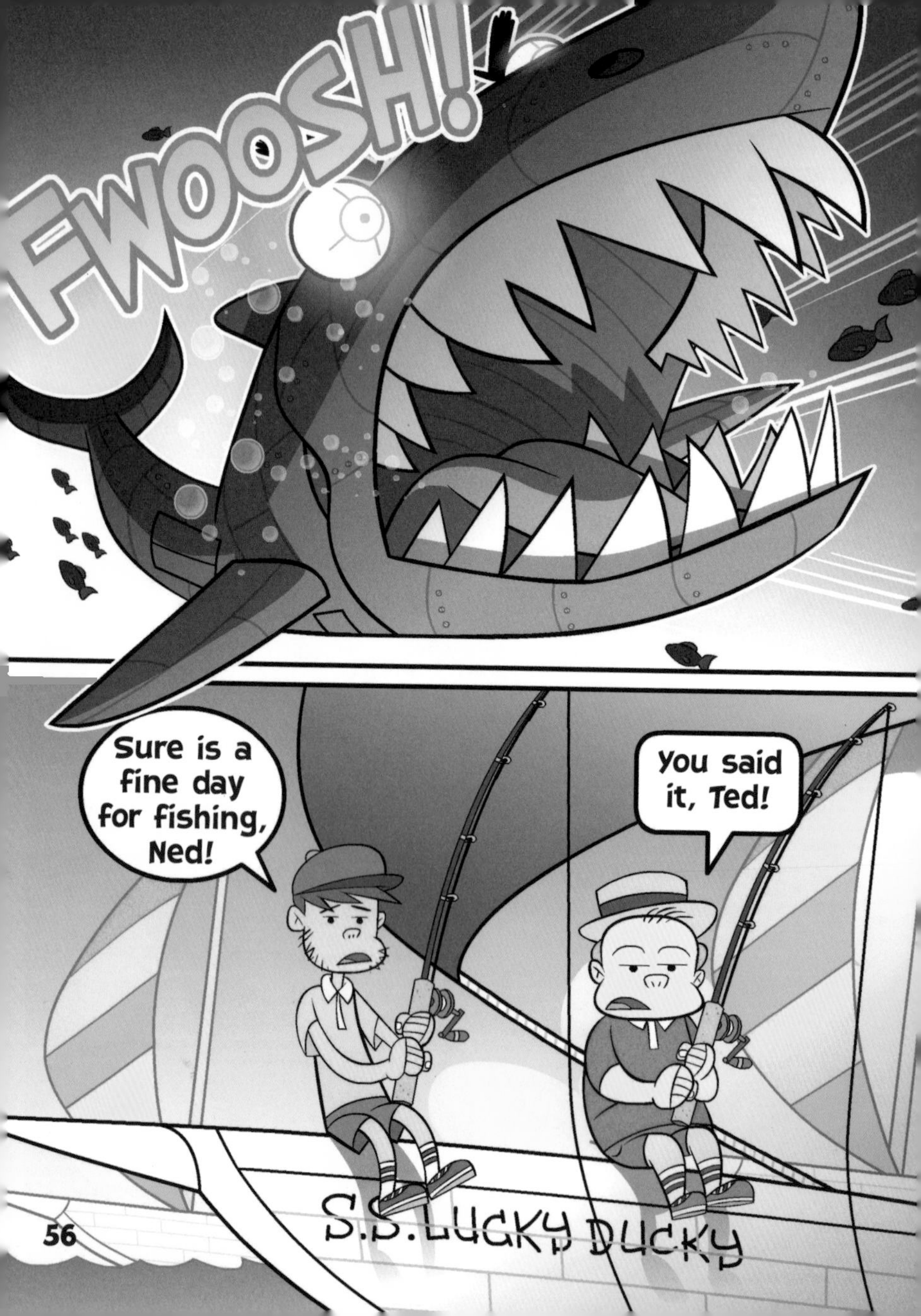
FWOOSH!
Sure is a fine day for fishing, Ned!
You said it, Ted!
S.S. LUCKY DUCKY

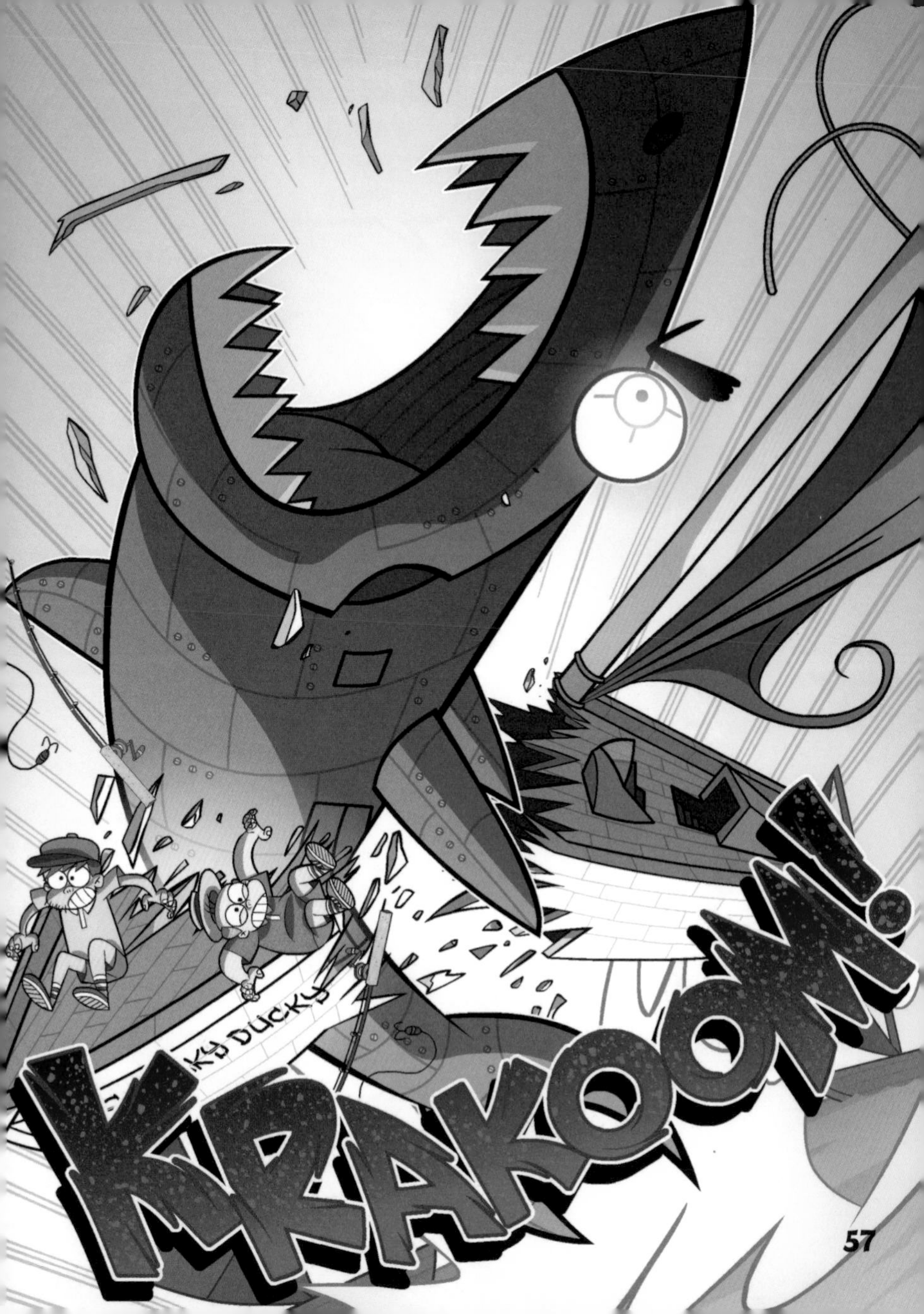
KY DUCKY
KRAKOOM!!

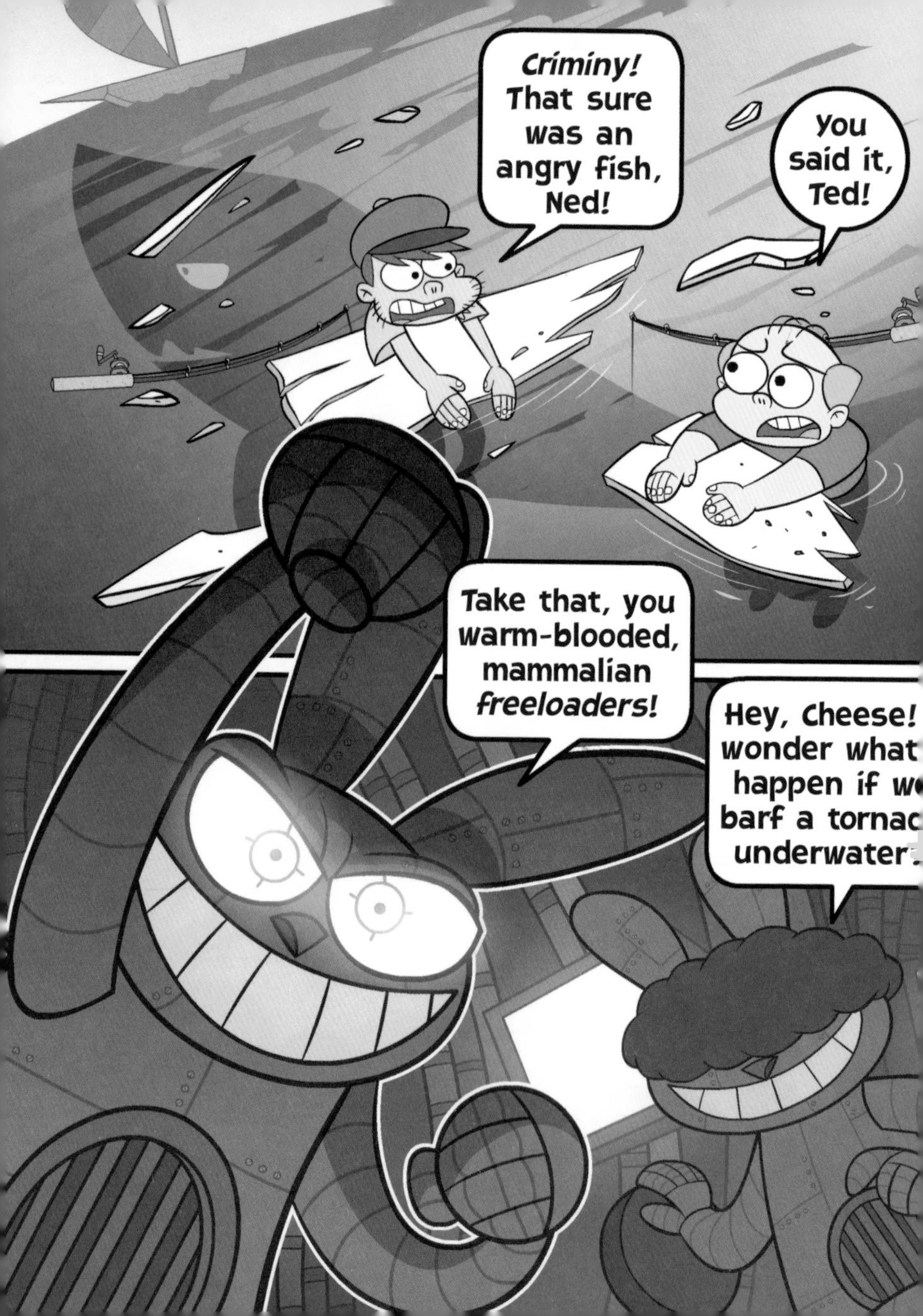
Criminy! That sure was an angry fish, Ned!
You said it, Ted!
Take that, you warm-blooded, mammalian freeloaders!
Hey, Cheese! wonder what happen if w barf a tornac underwater

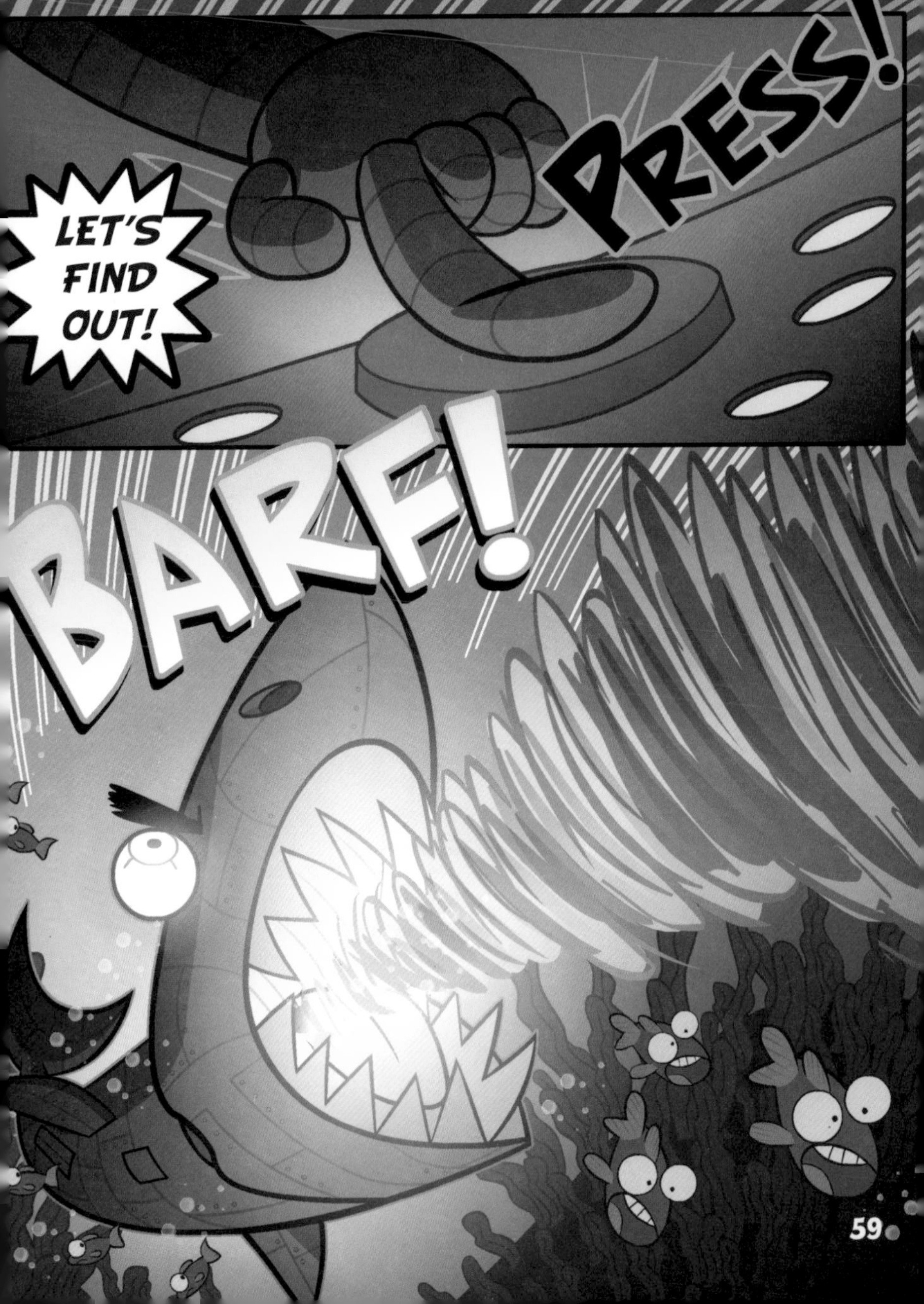
LET'S FIND OUT!
PRESS!
BARF!

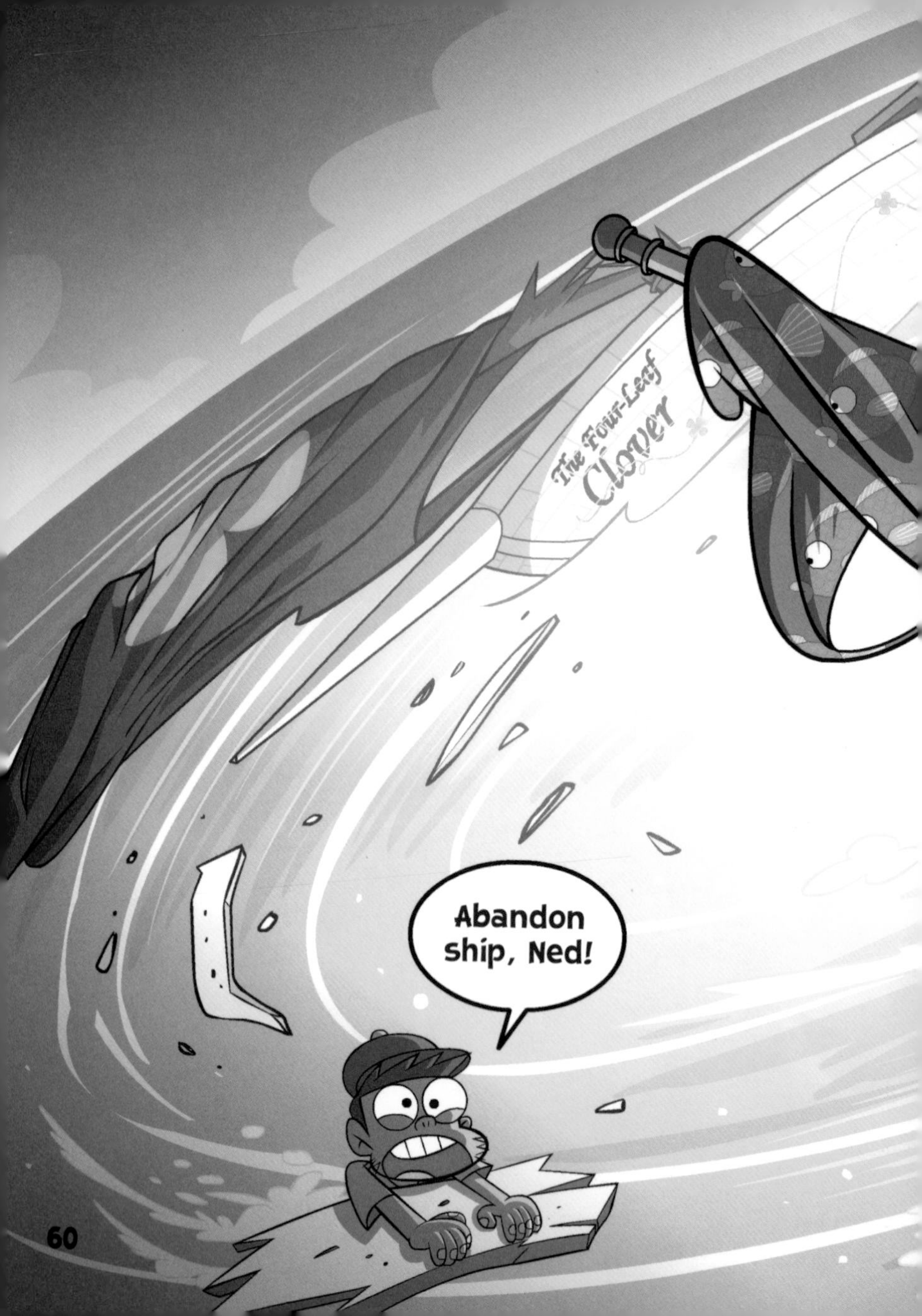
The Four-Leaf Clover
Abandon ship, Ned!

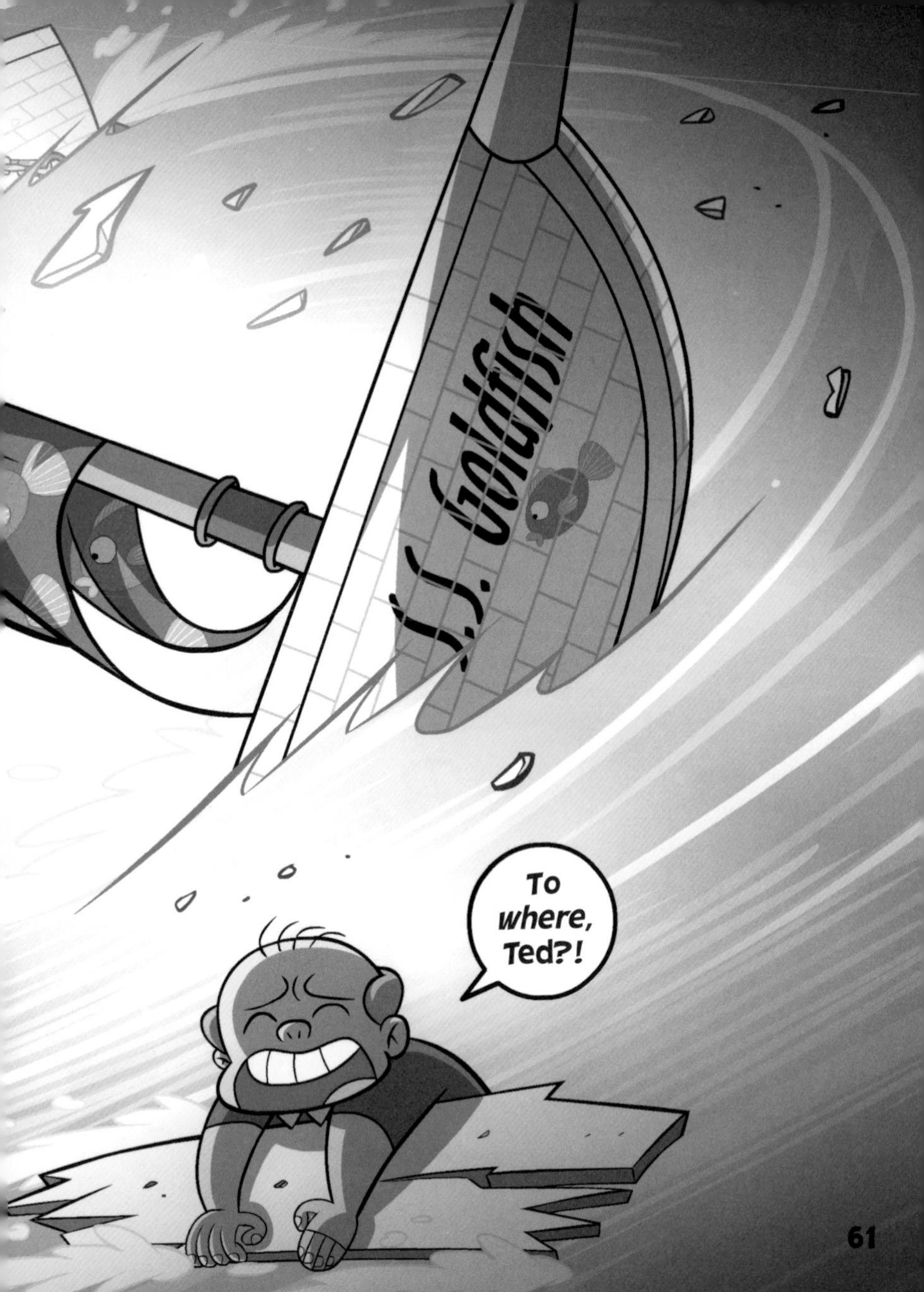
S.S. Goldfish
To where, Ted?!

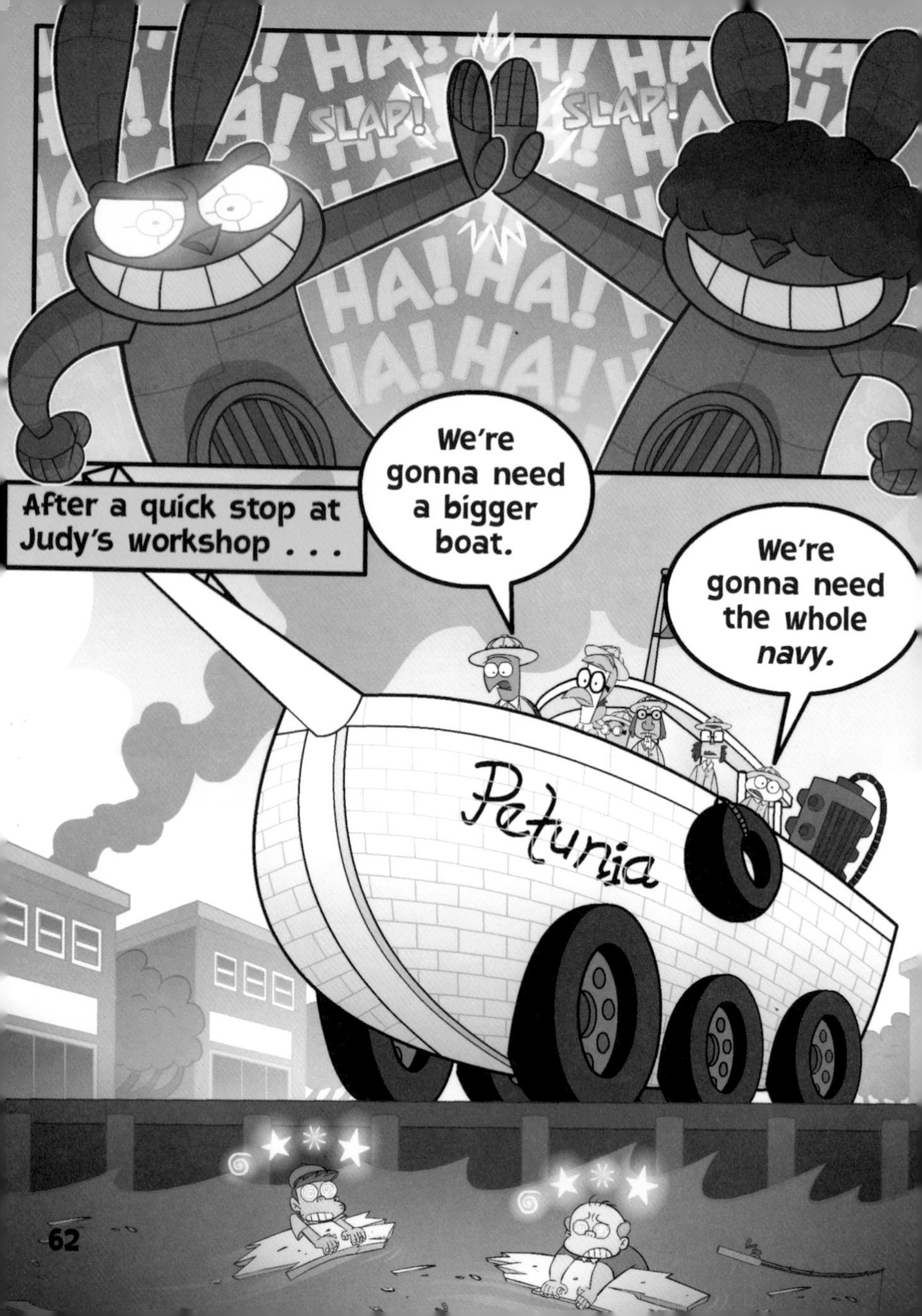
HA! HA! HA! HA!
SLAP!
SLAP!
HA! HA! HA! HA!
After a quick stop at Judy's workshop . . .
We're gonna need a bigger boat.
We're gonna need the whole *navy.*
Petunia

63

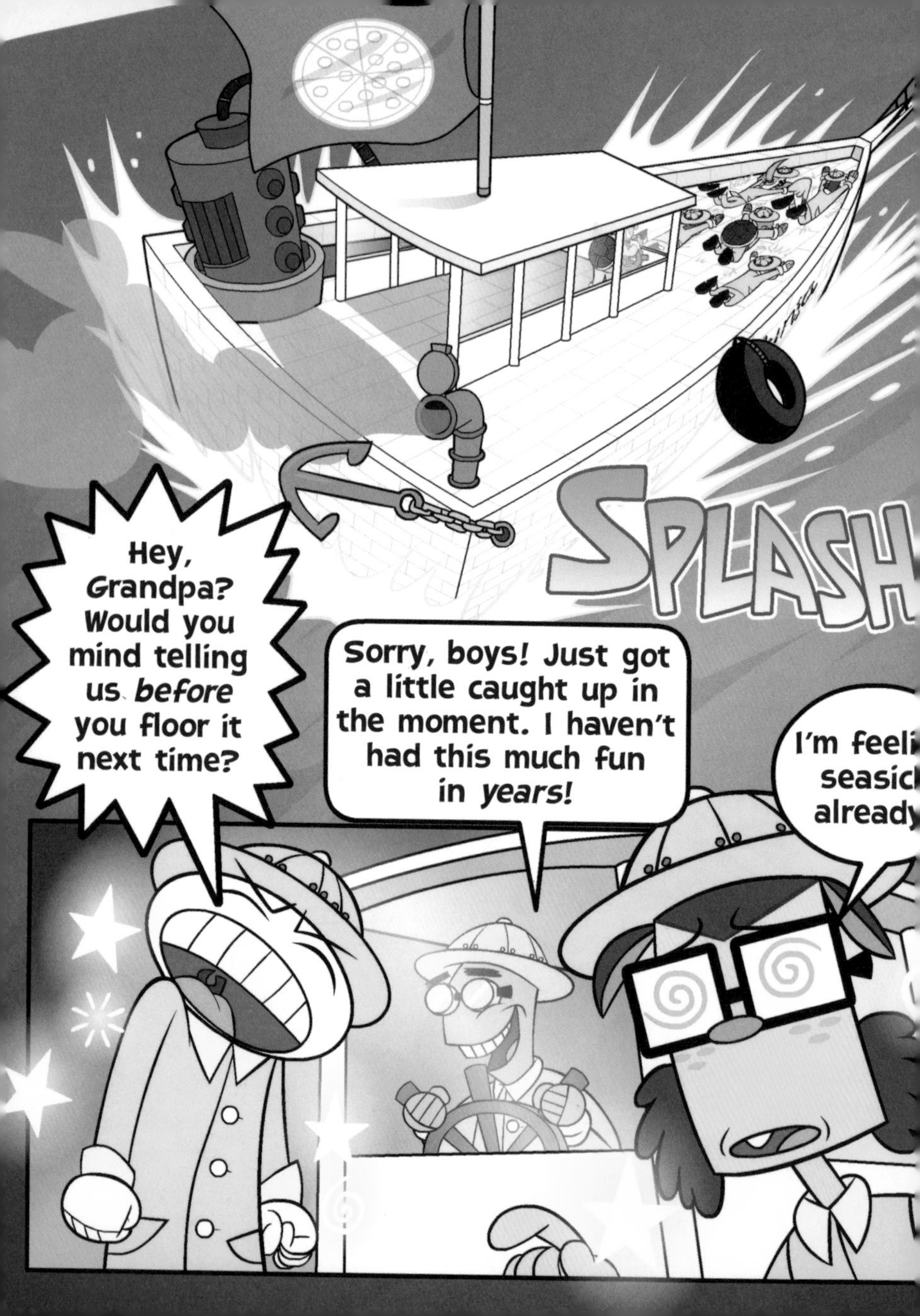
SPLASH
Hey, Grandpa? Would you mind telling us *before* you floor it next time?
Sorry, boys! Just got a little caught up in the moment. I haven't had this much fun in *years*!

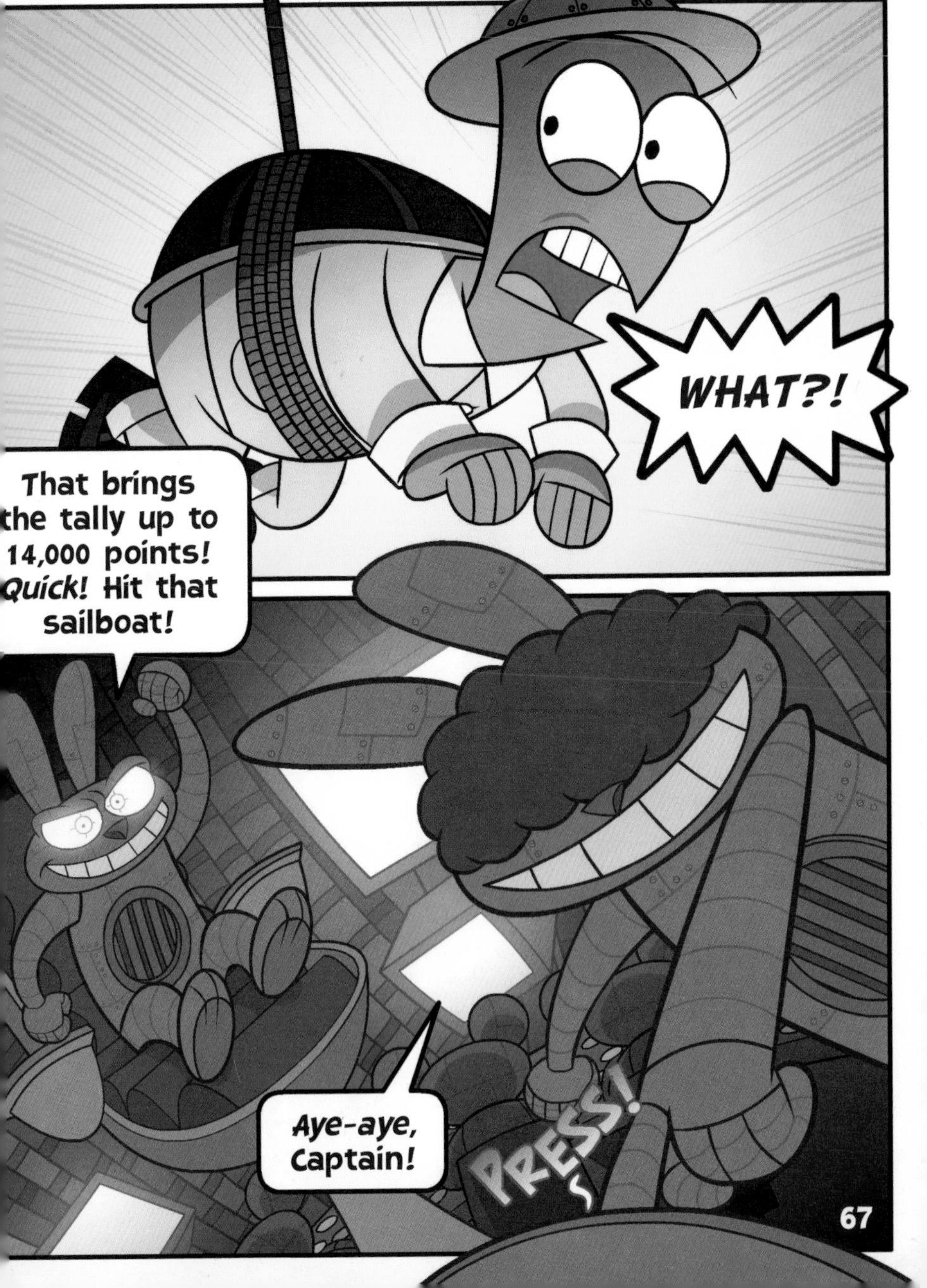
WHAT?!
That brings the tally up to 14,000 points! *Quick!* Hit that sailboat!
Aye-aye, Captain!
PRESS!

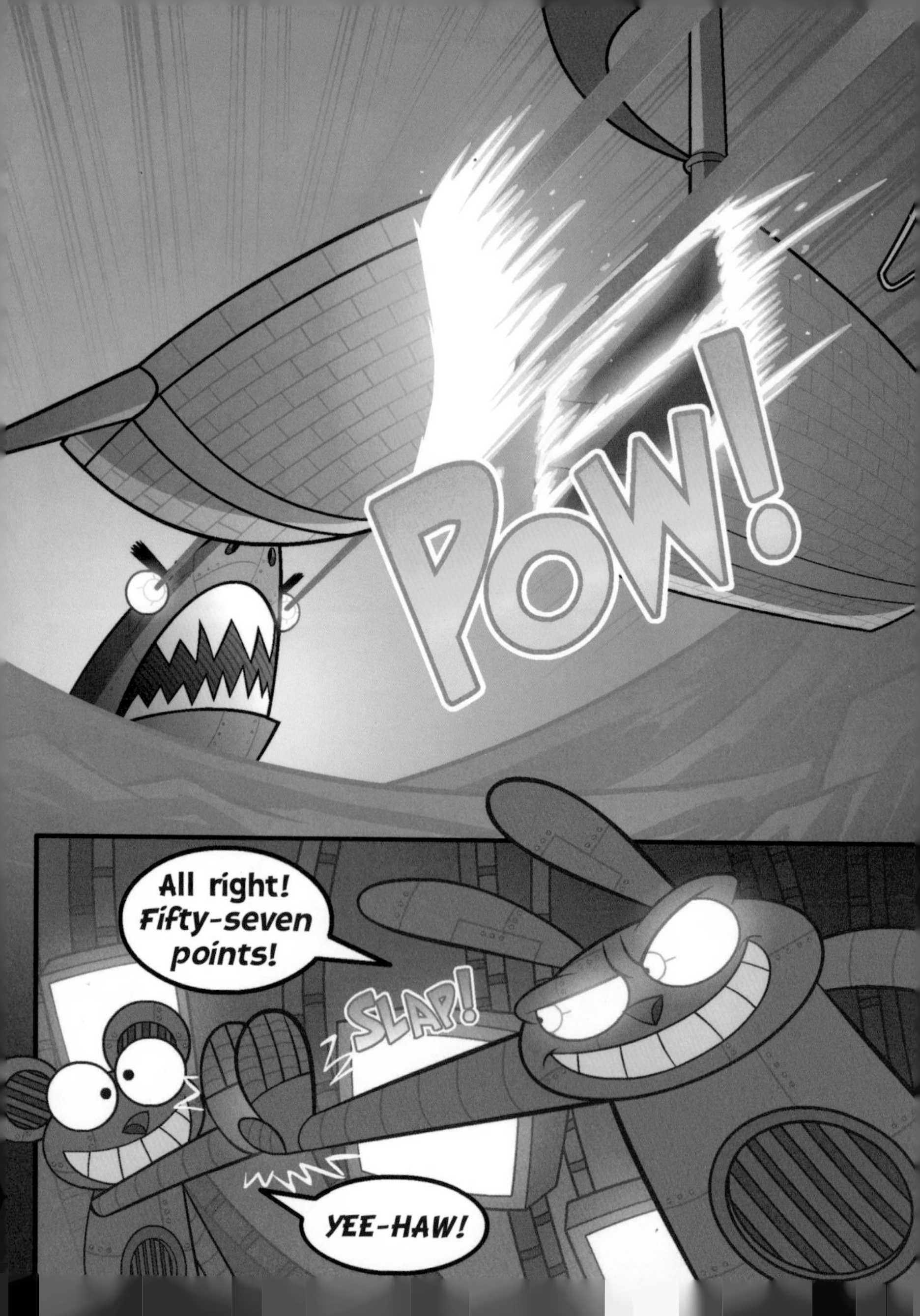
POW!
All right! Fifty-seven points!
SLAP!
YEE-HAW!

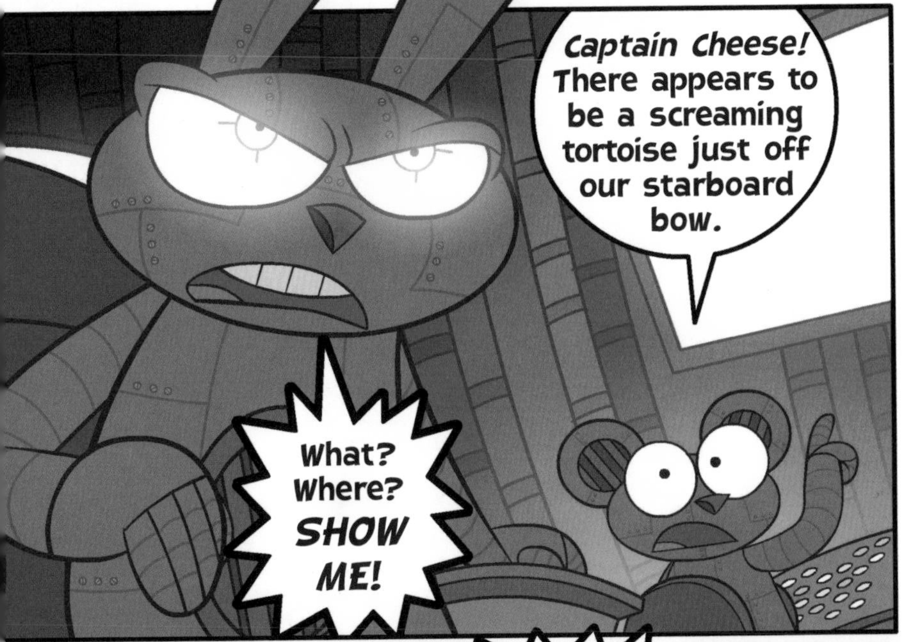
Captain Cheese! There appears to be a screaming tortoise just off our starboard bow.
What? Where? SHOW ME!
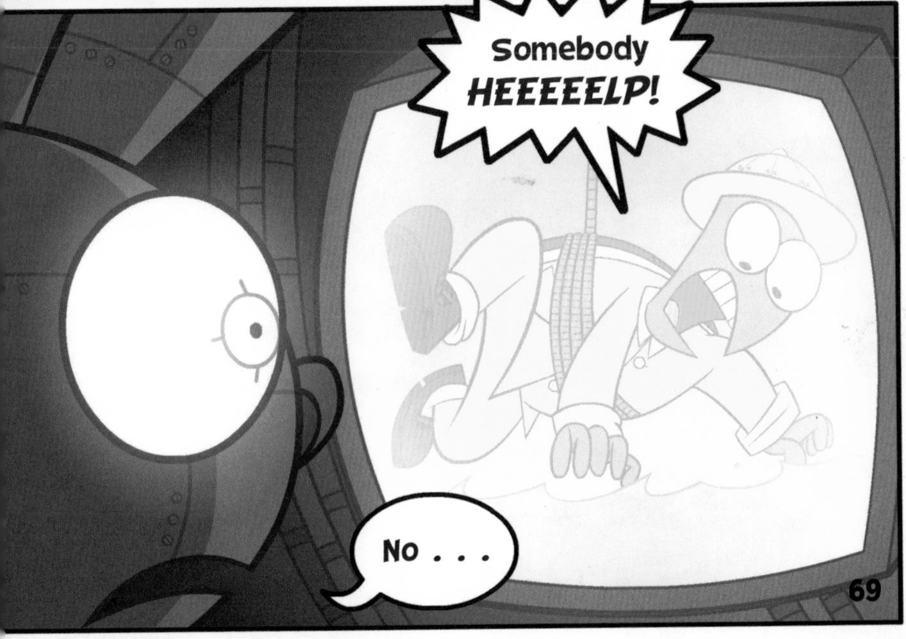
Somebody HEEEEELP!
No . . .

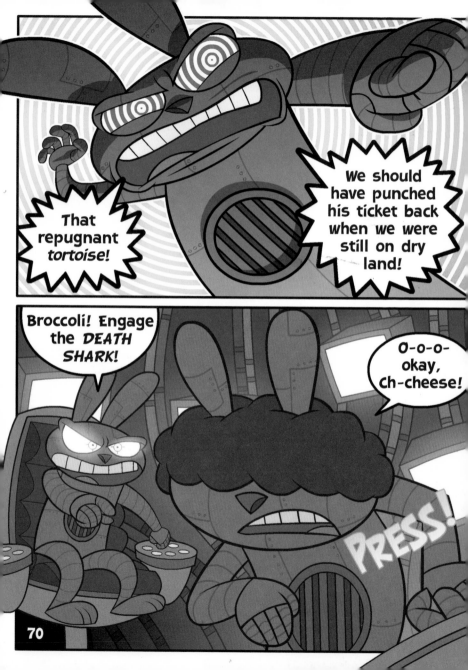

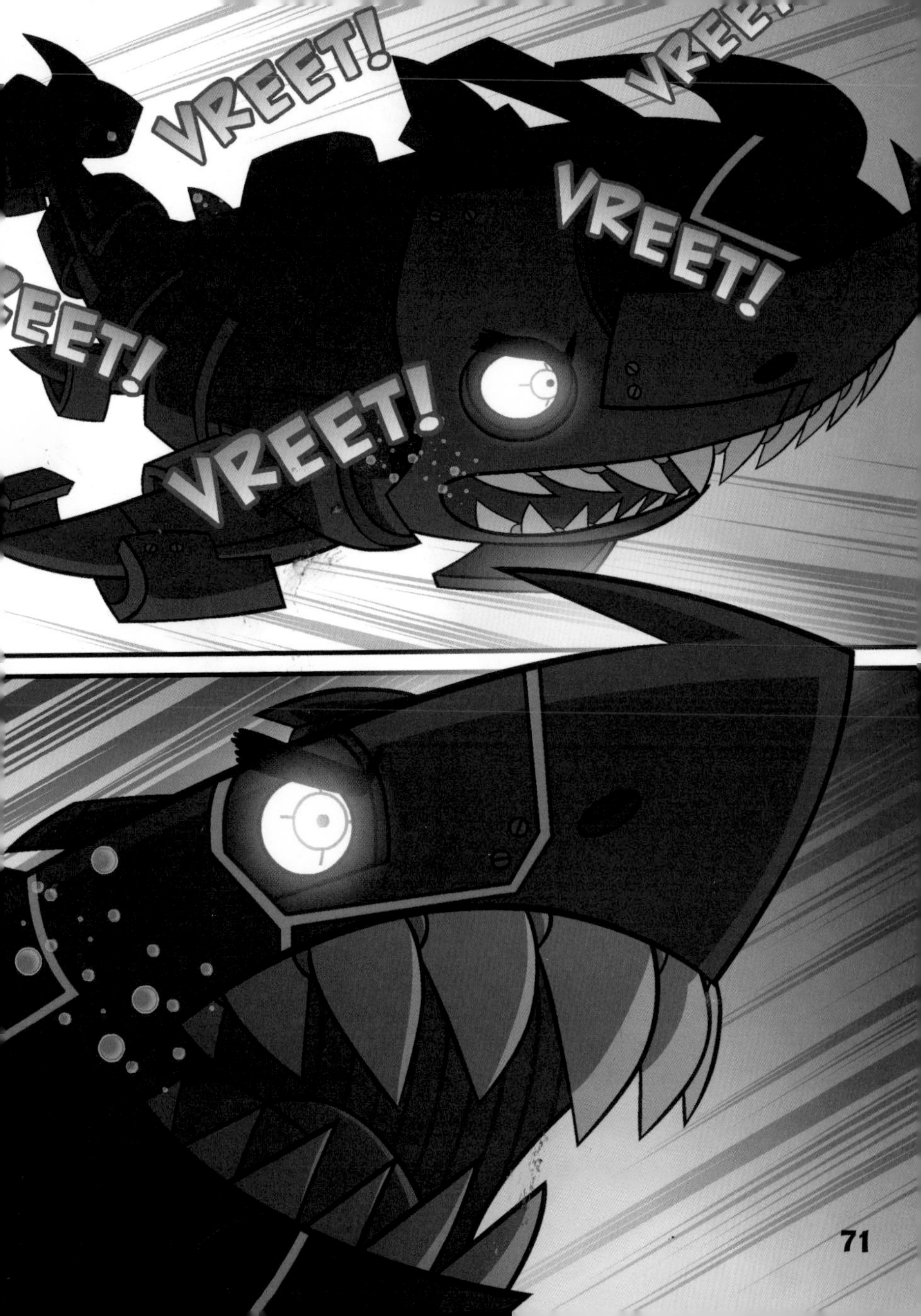
VREET!
VREET!
VREET!

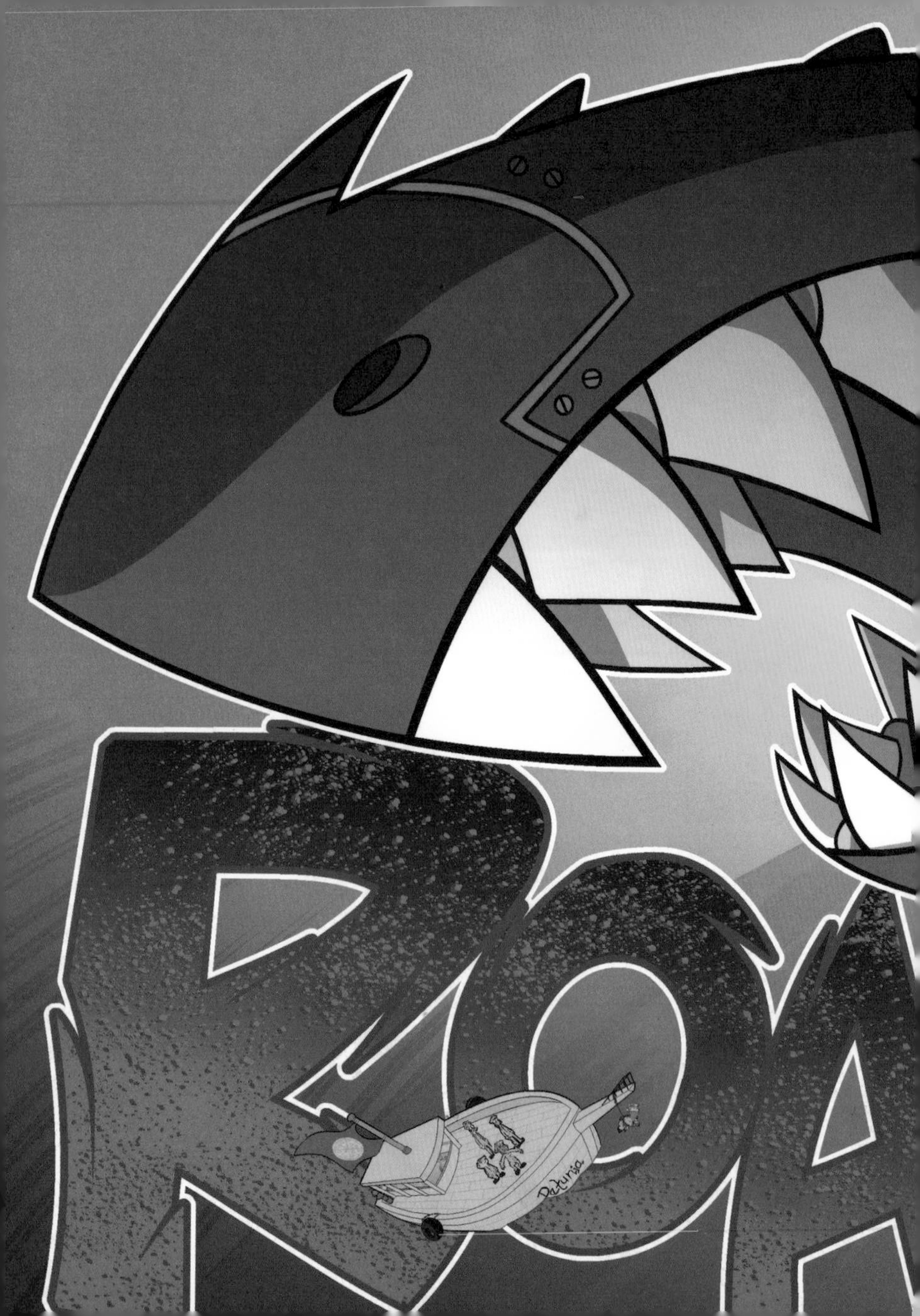

ROA
Petunia

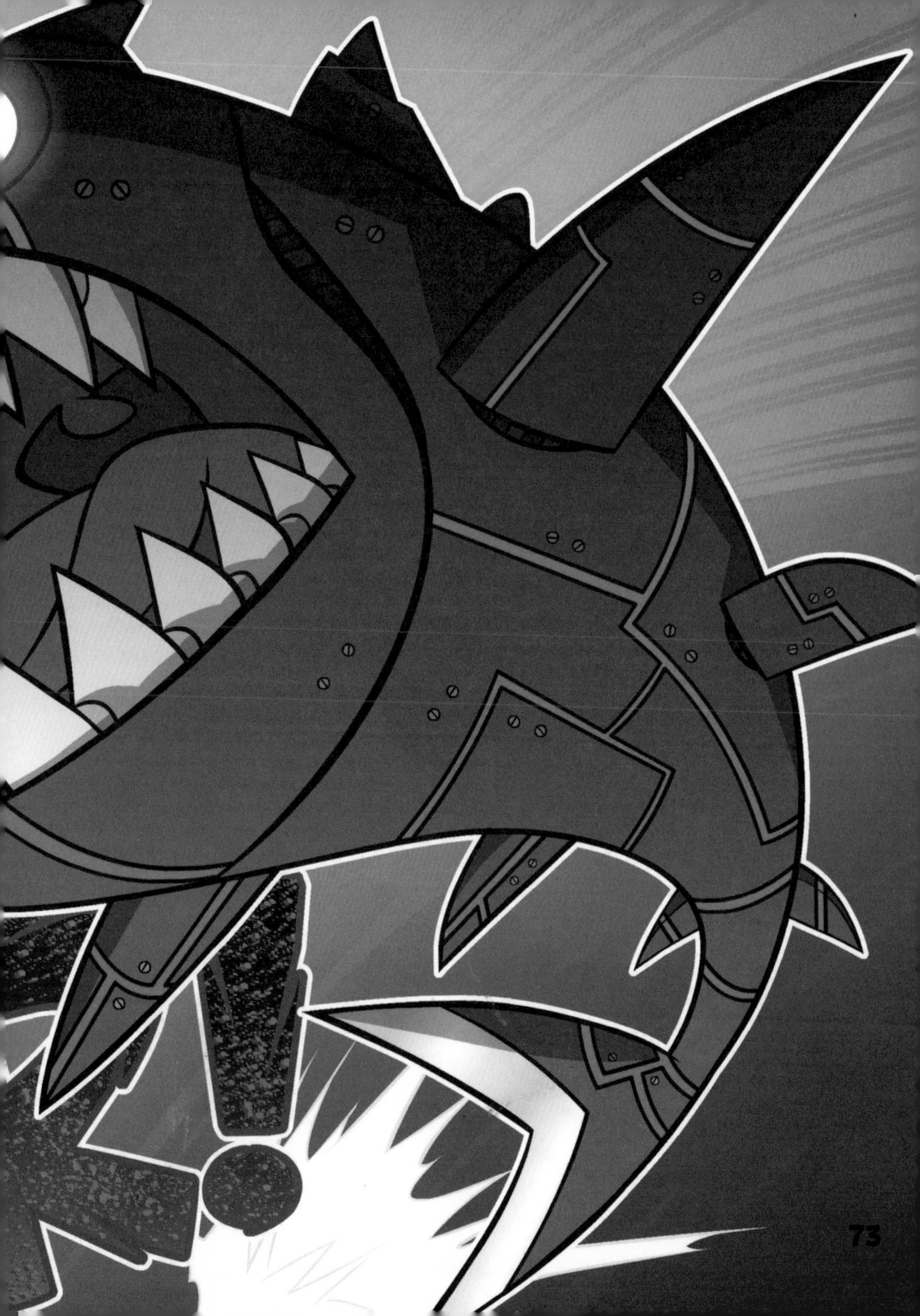

74

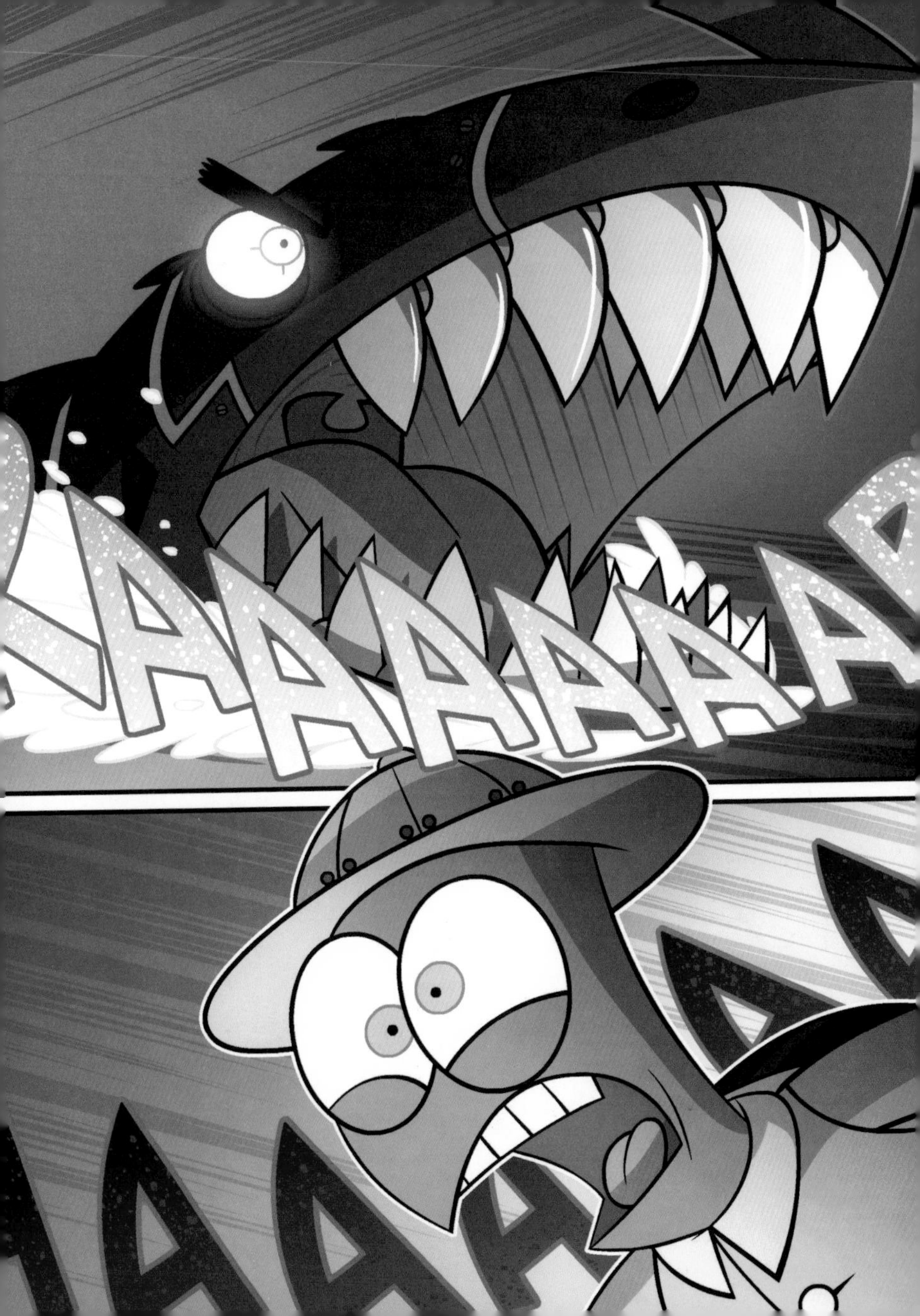

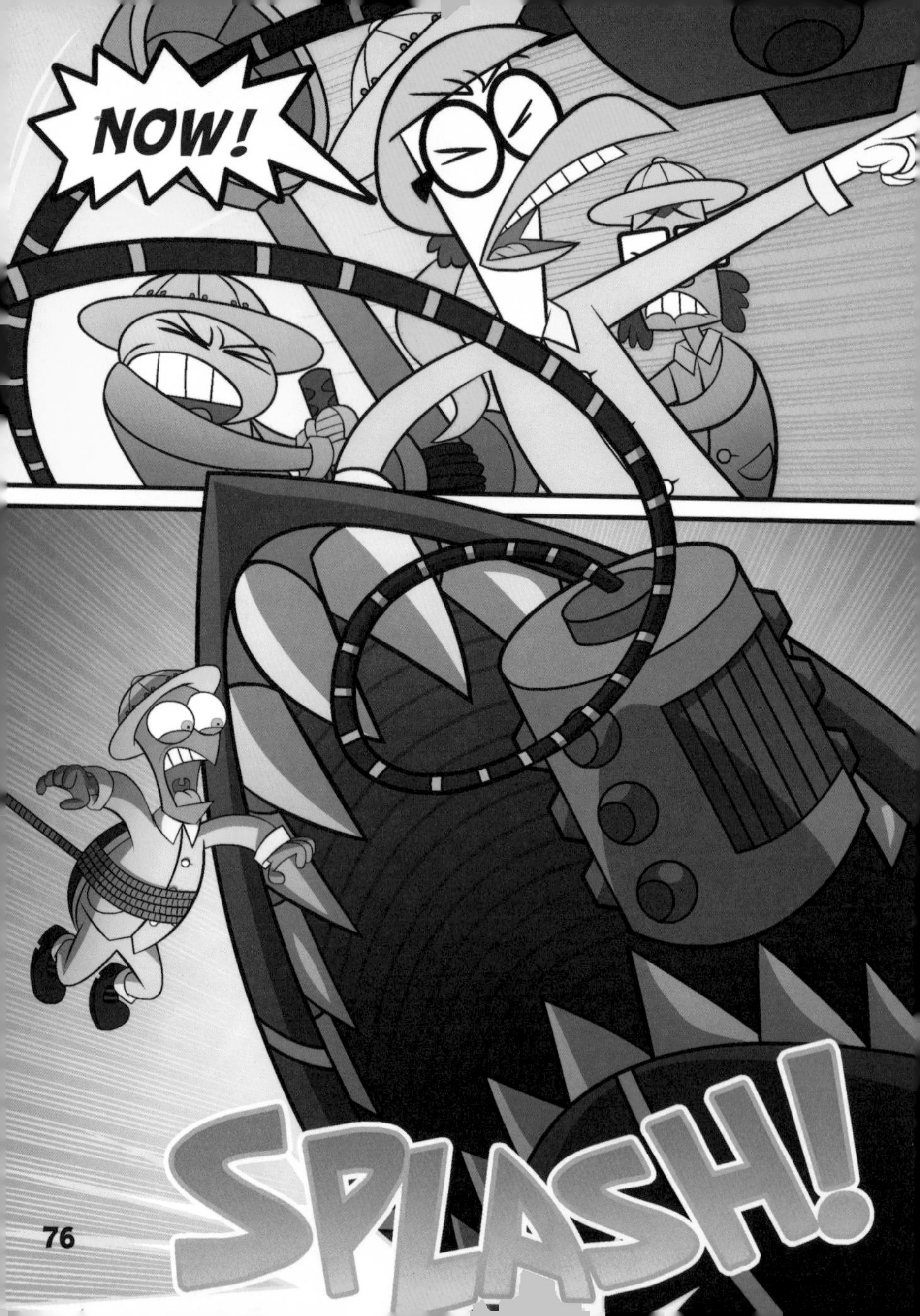
NOW!
SPLASH!

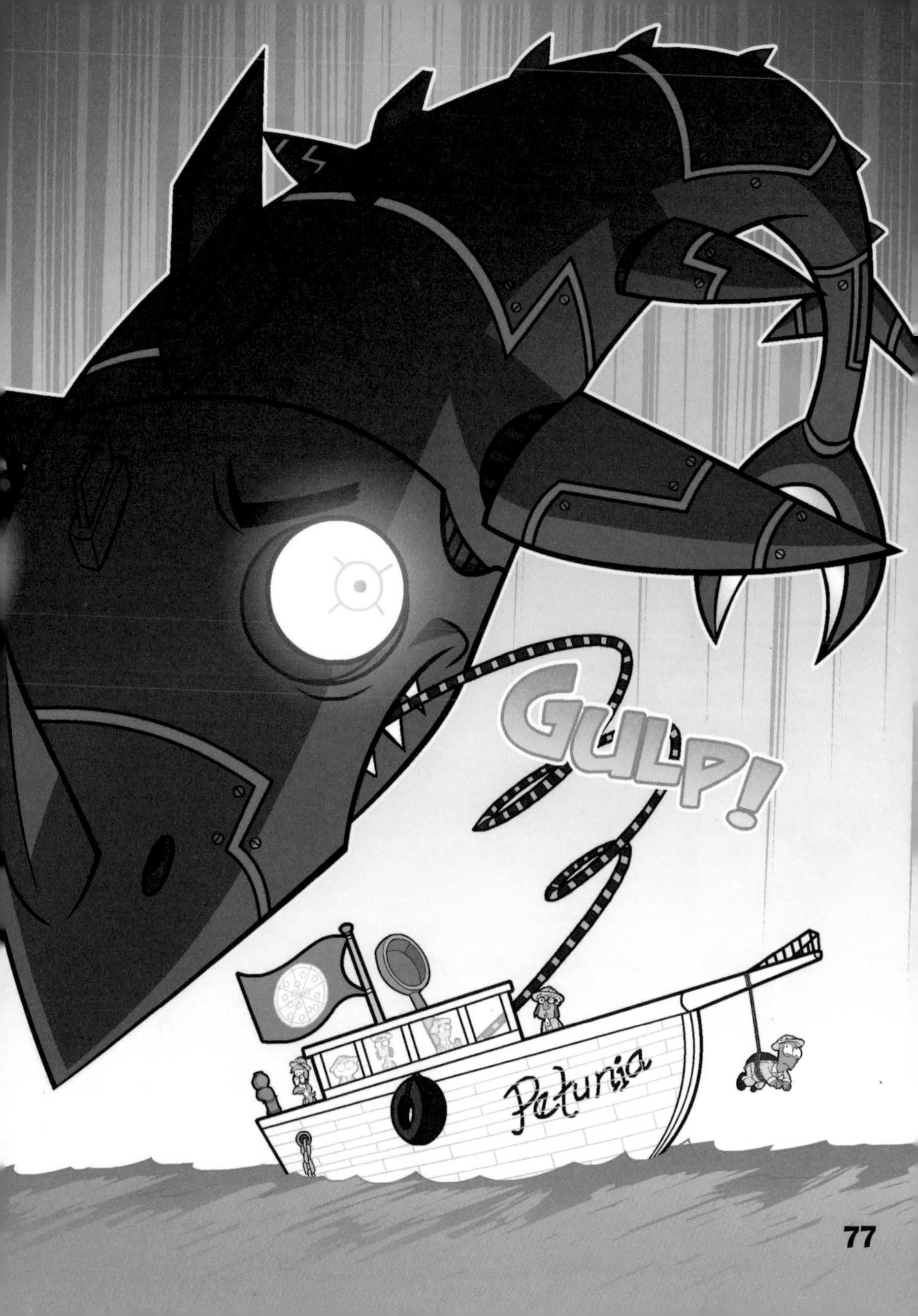
GULP!
Petunia

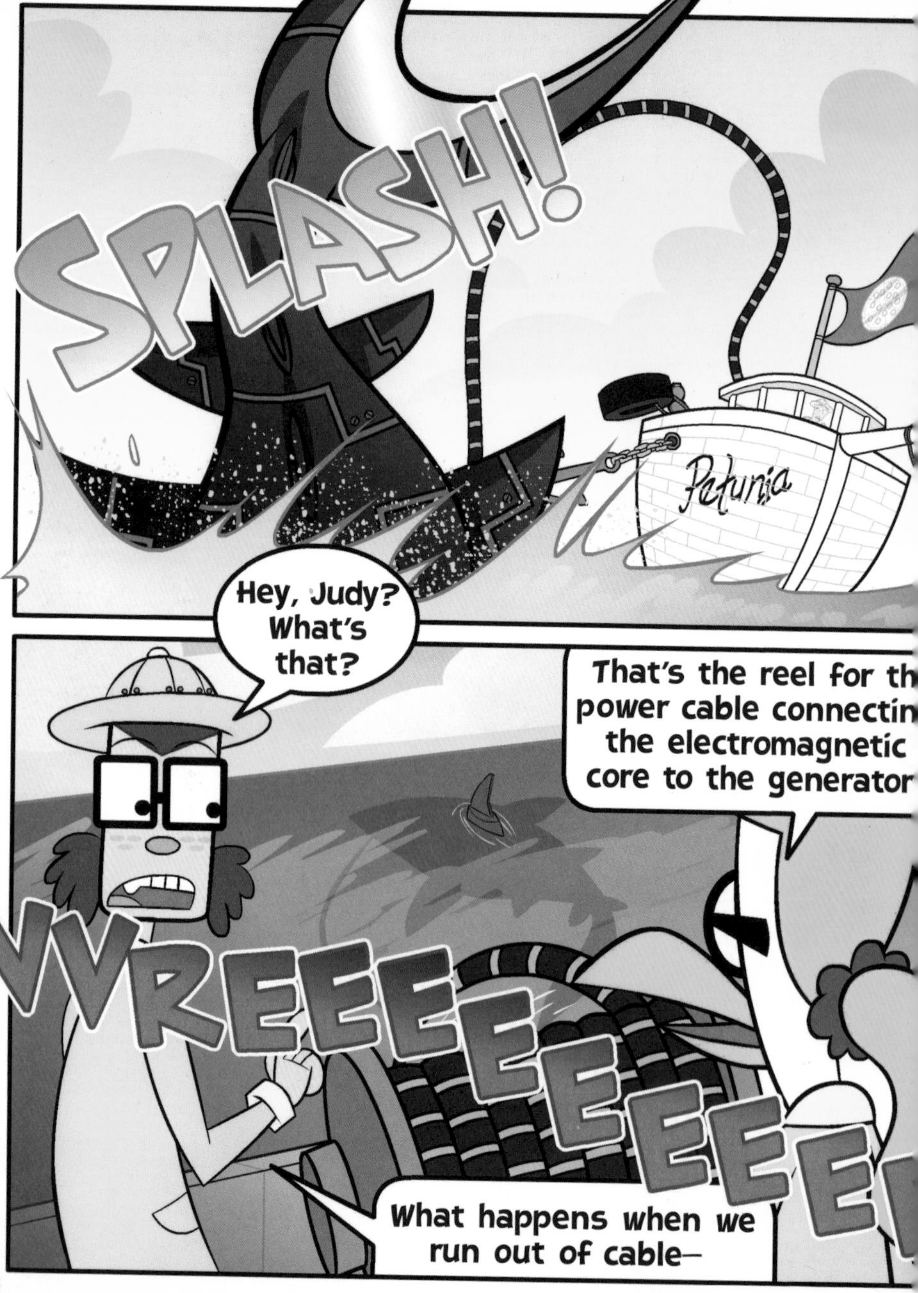
SPLASH!
Petunia
Hey, Judy? What's that?
That's the reel for th power cable connectin the electromagnetic core to the generator
VVREEEEEEEEE
What happens when we run out of cable—

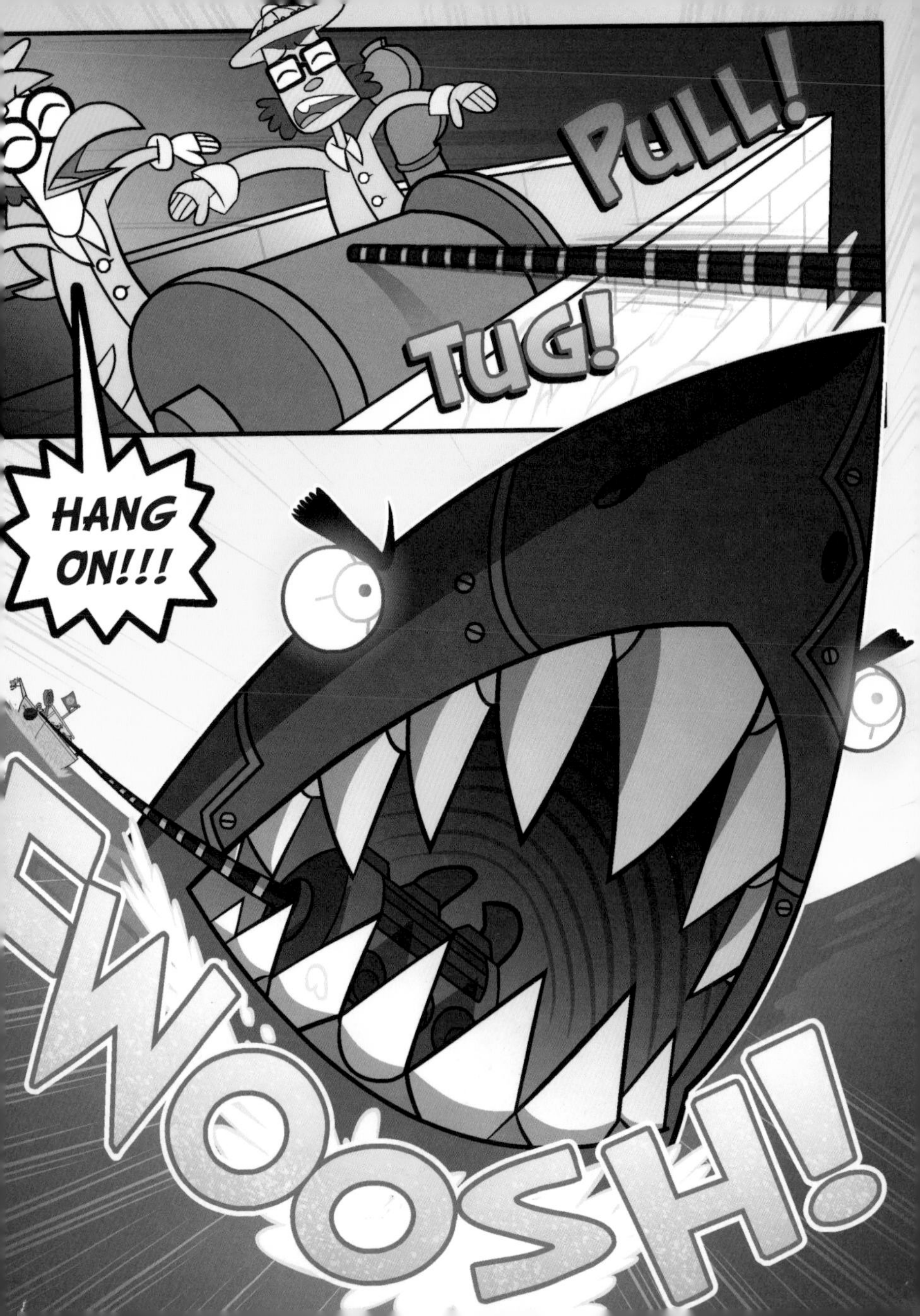
PULL!
TUG!
HANG ON!!!
WOOSH!

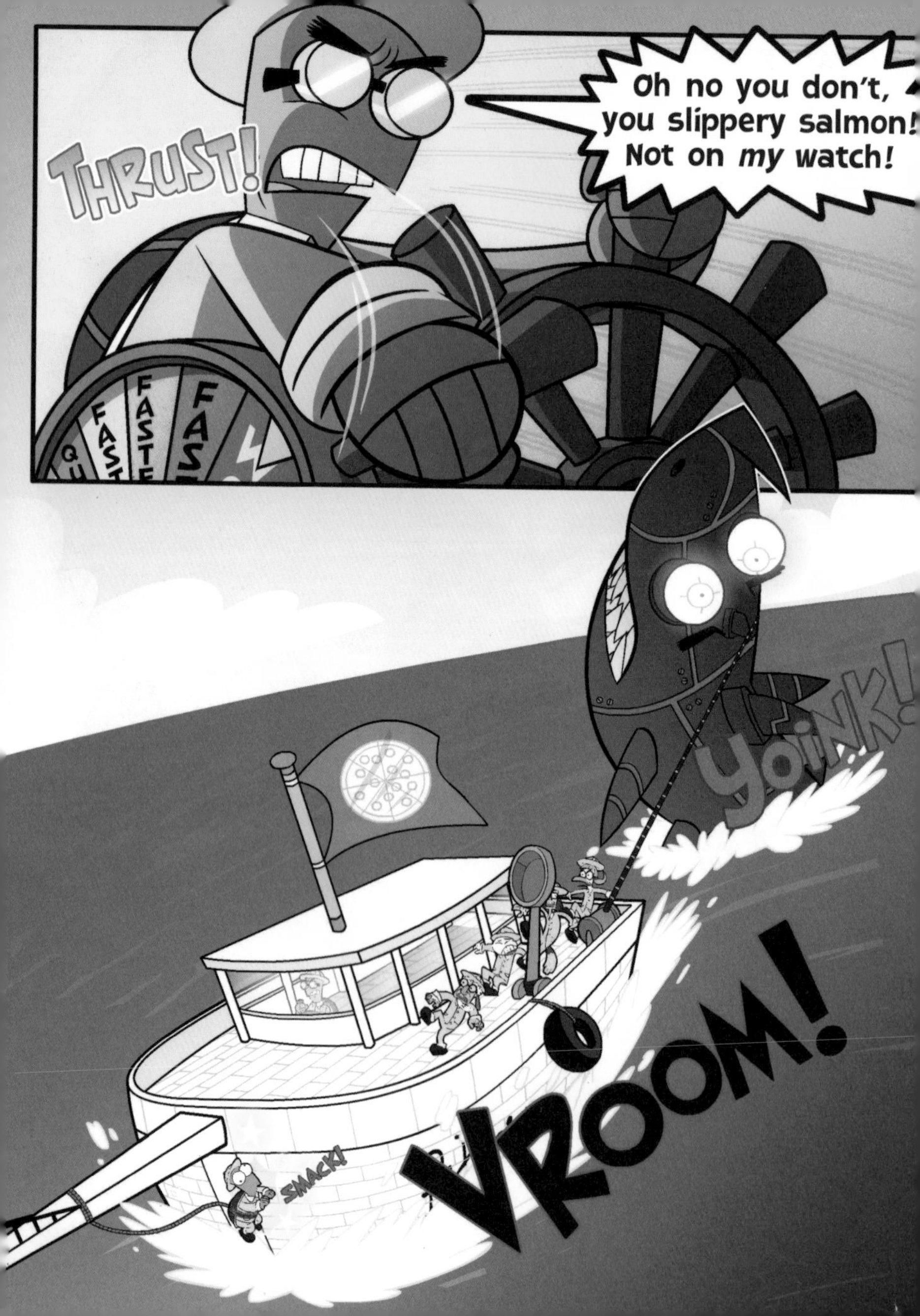
Oh no you don't, you slippery salmon! Not on *my* watch!
THRUST!
YOINK!
SMACK!
VROOM!

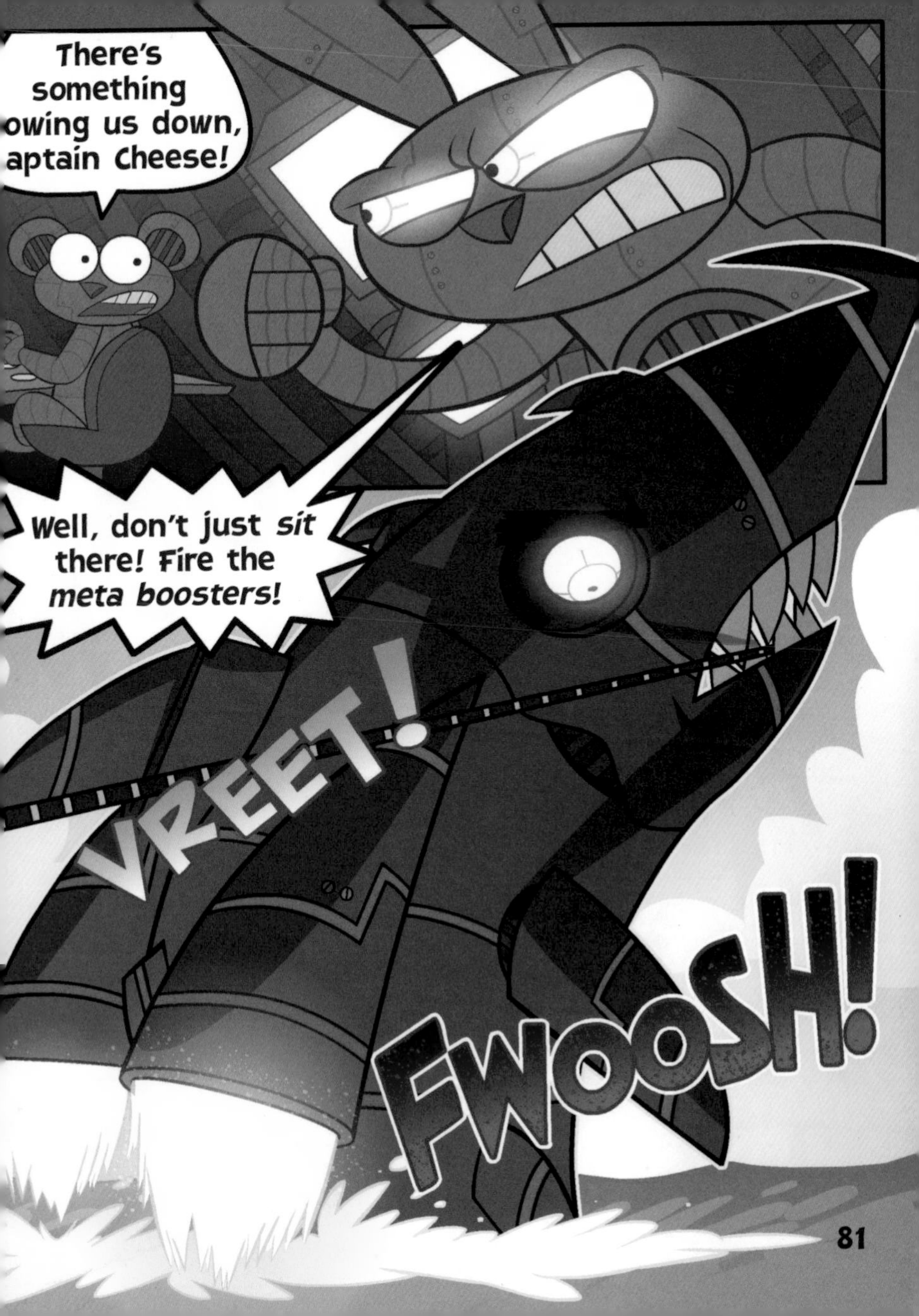
There's something owing us down, aptain Cheese!
Well, don't just *sit* there! Fire the *meta boosters!*
VREET!
FWOOSH!

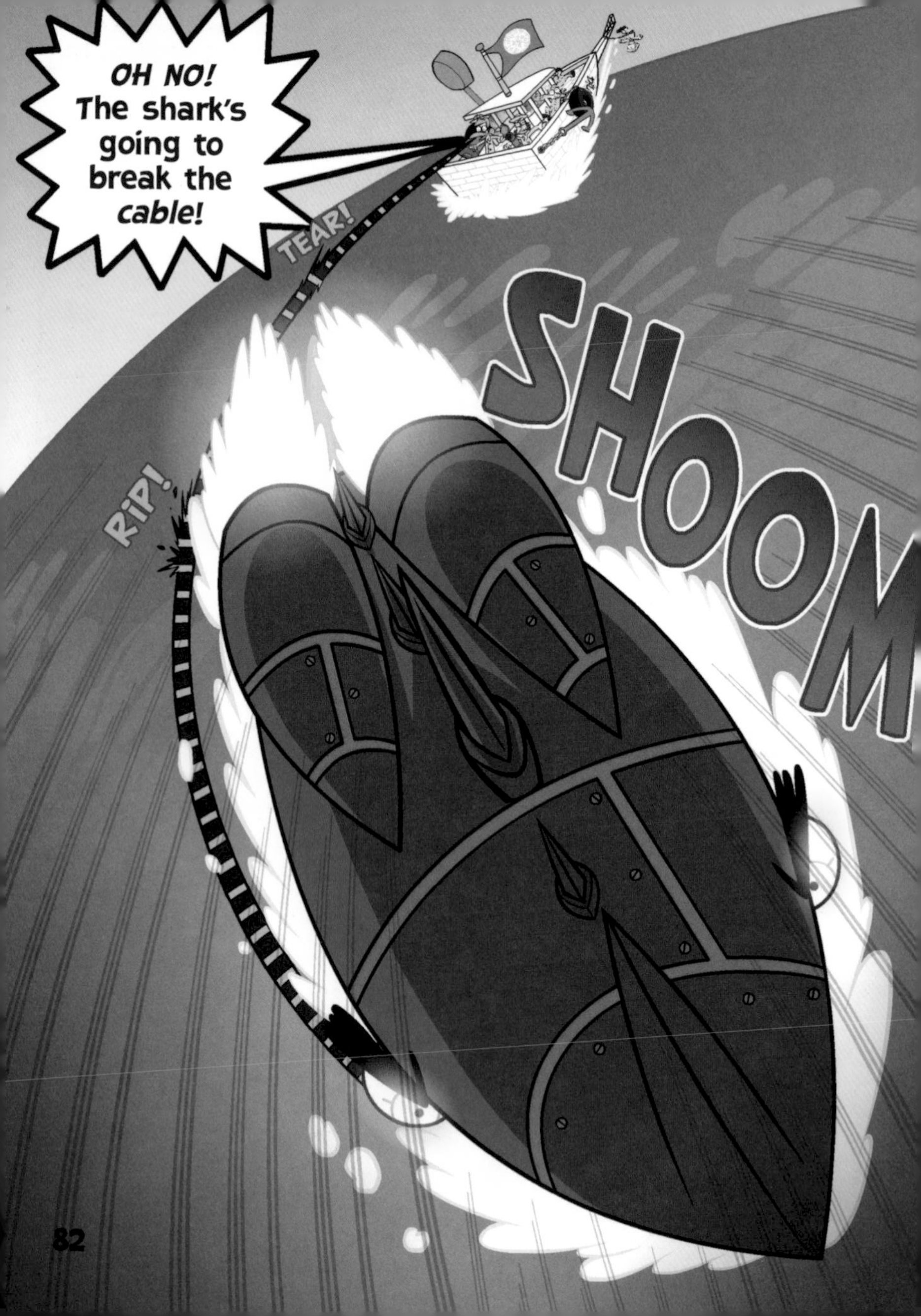
OH NO! The shark's going to break the cable!
TEAR!
RIP!
SHOOM

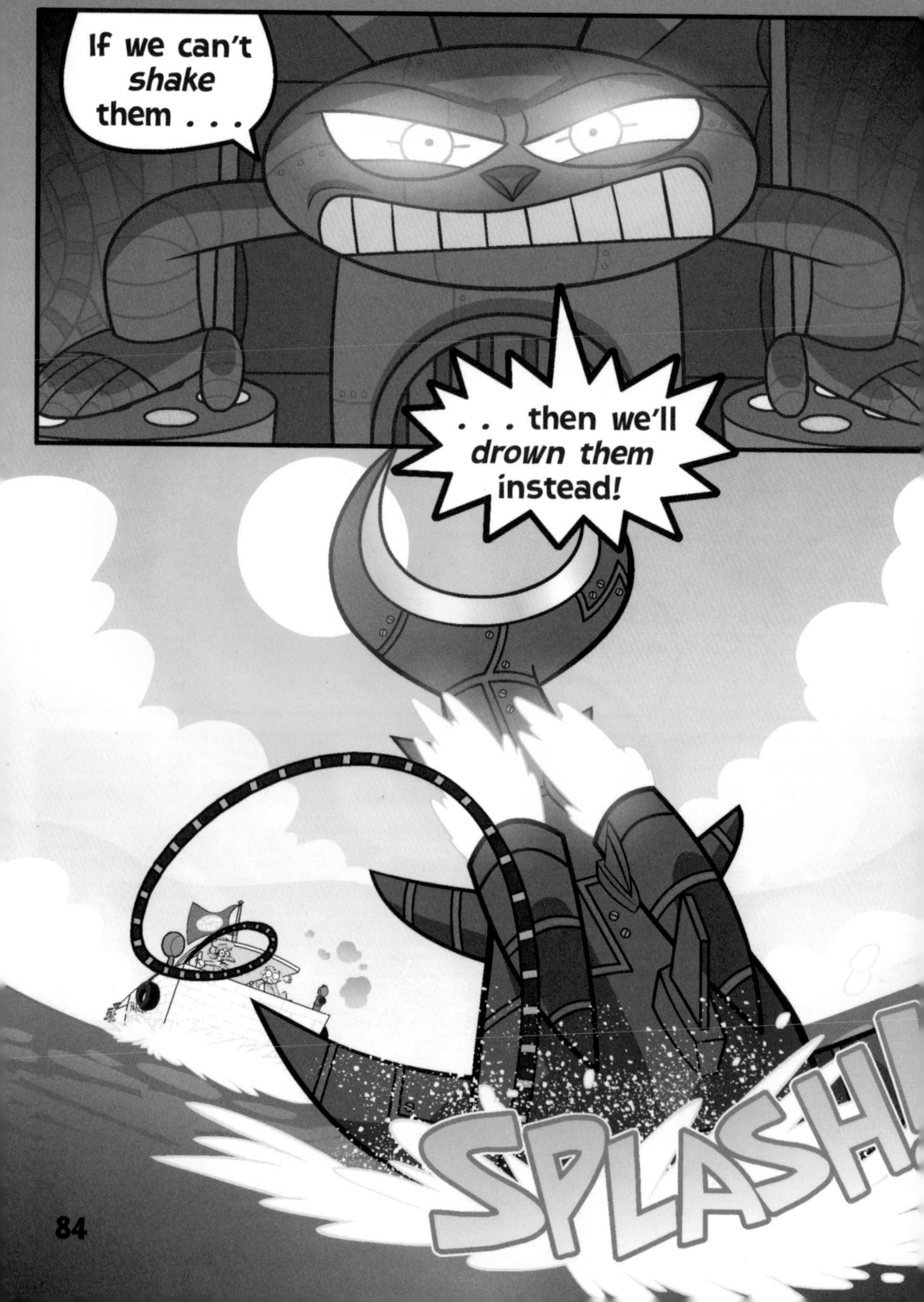
If we can't *shake* them . . .
. . . then we'll *drown them* instead!
SPLASH!

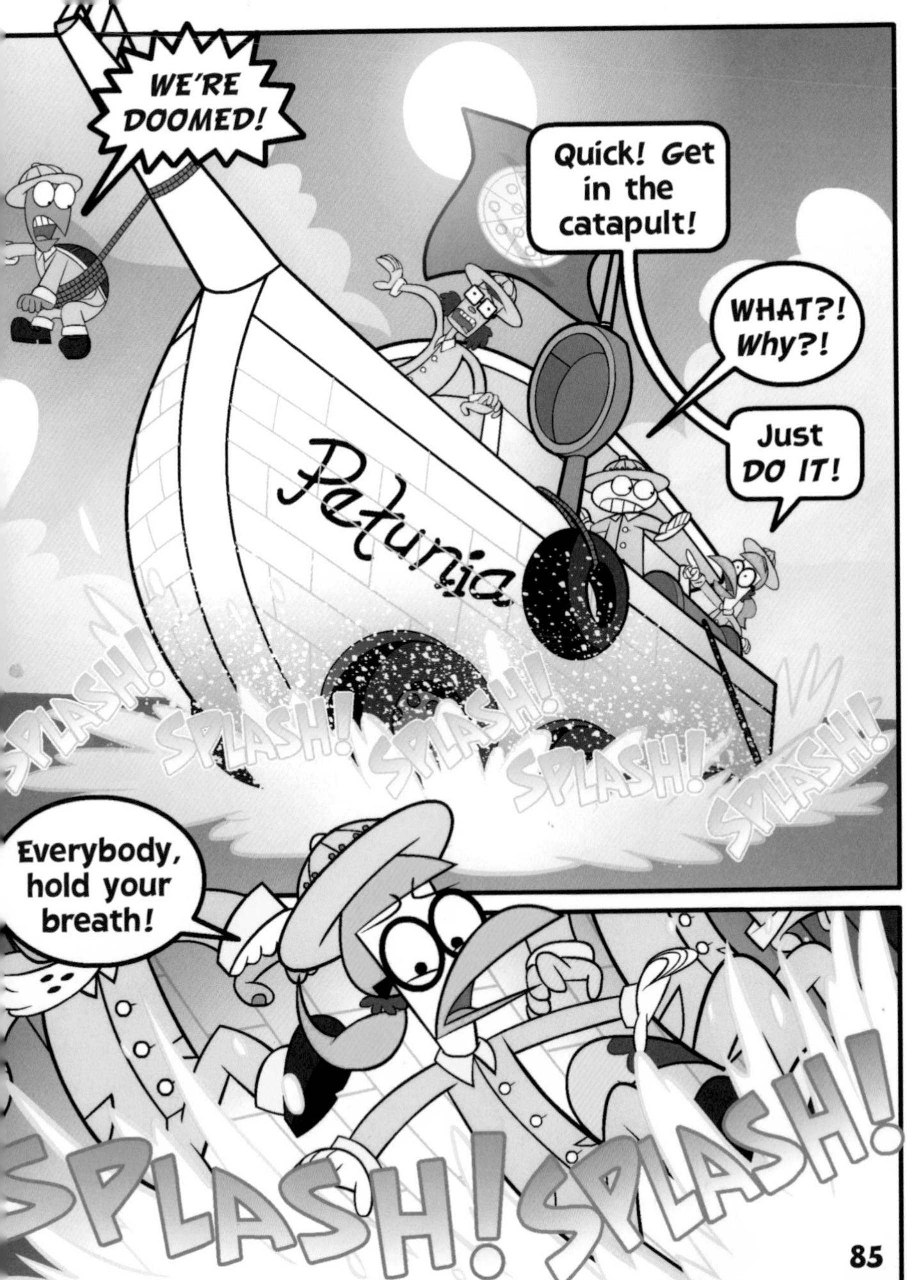
WE'RE DOOMED!
Quick! Get in the catapult!
WHAT?! Why?!
Just DO IT!
Petunia
SPLASH! SPLASH! SPLASH! SPLASH! SPLASH!
Everybody, hold your breath!
SPLASH! SPLASH!

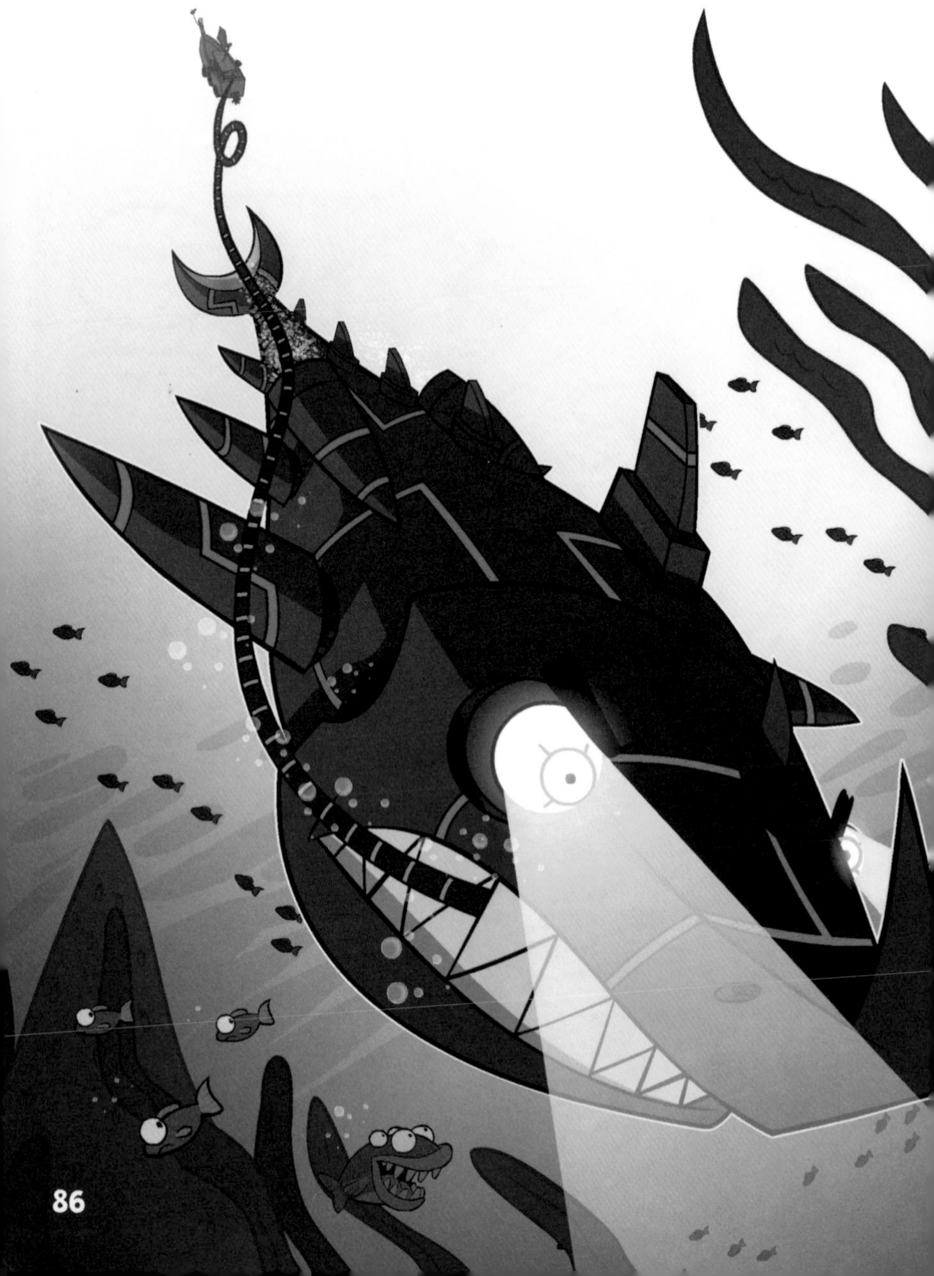

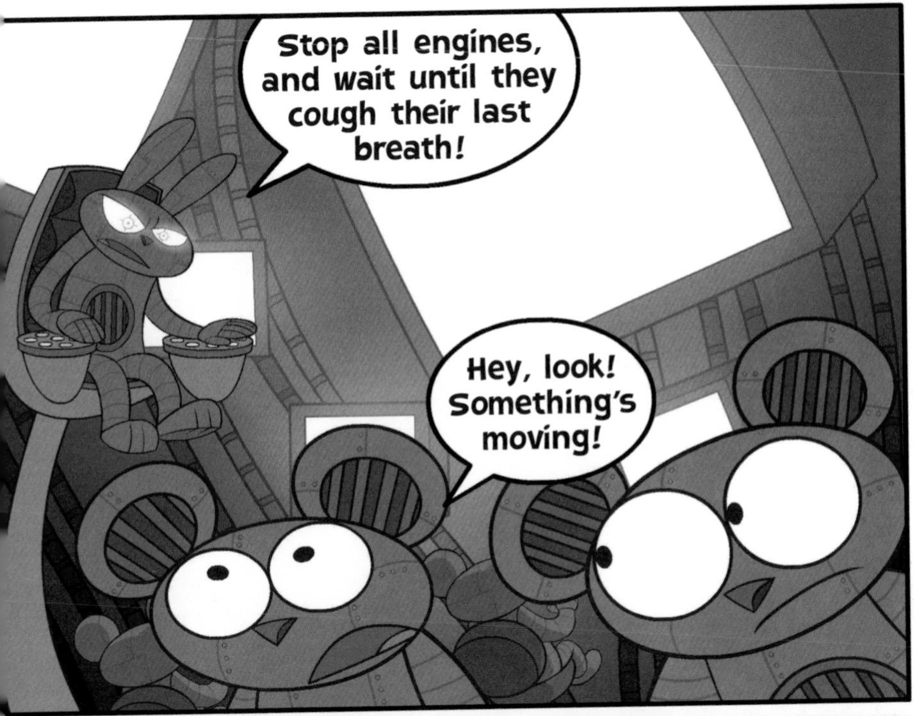
Stop all engines, and wait until they cough their last breath!
Hey, look! Something's moving!

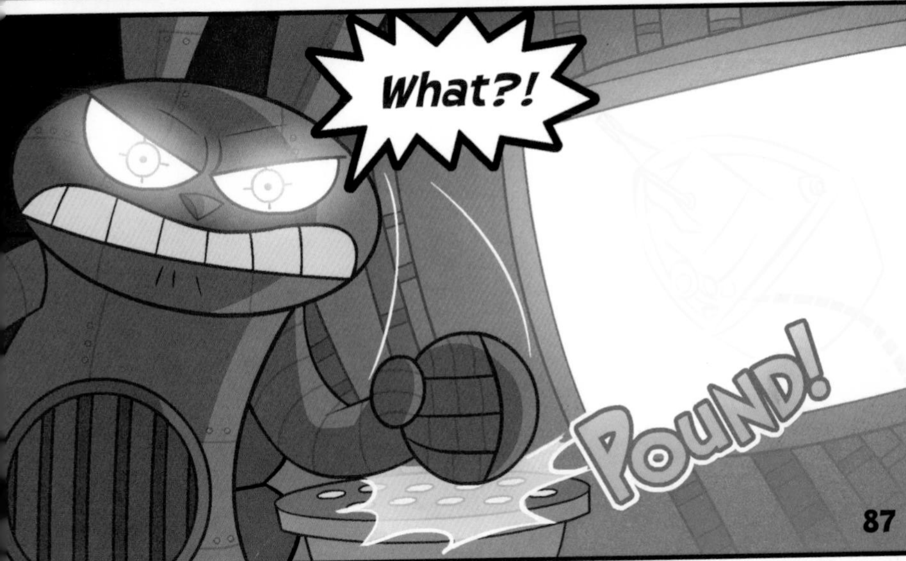
What?!
POUND!

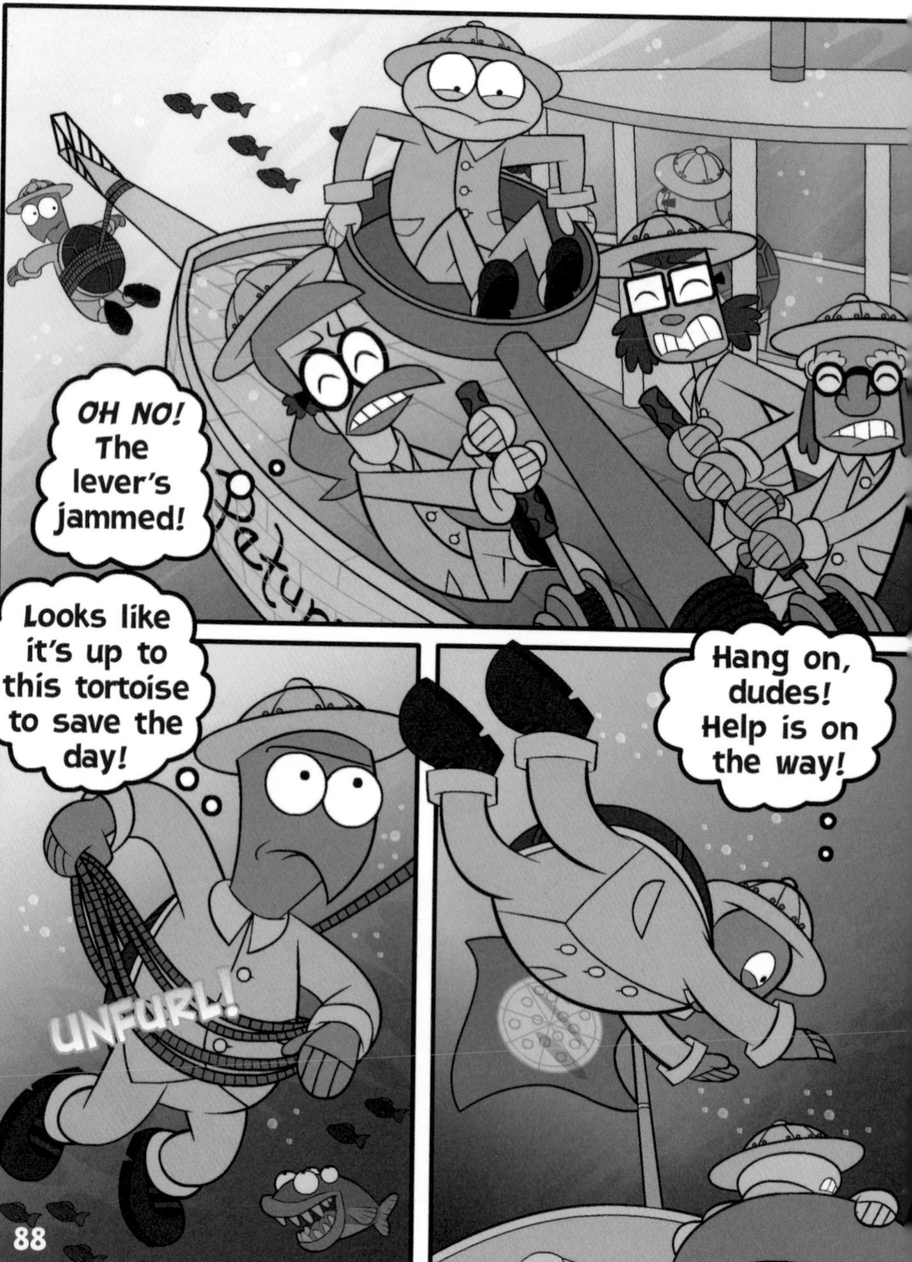

OH NO! The lever's jammed!
Looks like it's up to this tortoise to save the day!
UNFURL!
Hang on, dudes! Help is on the way!

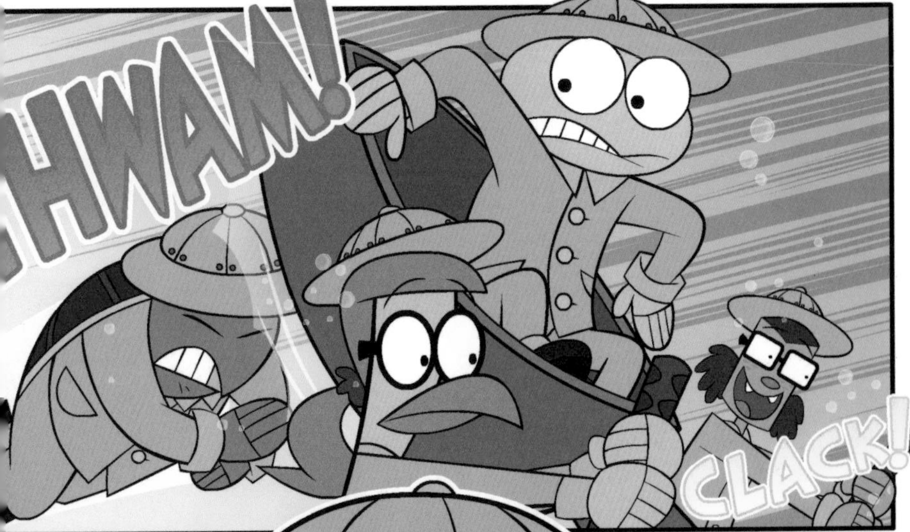
HWAM!
CLACK!

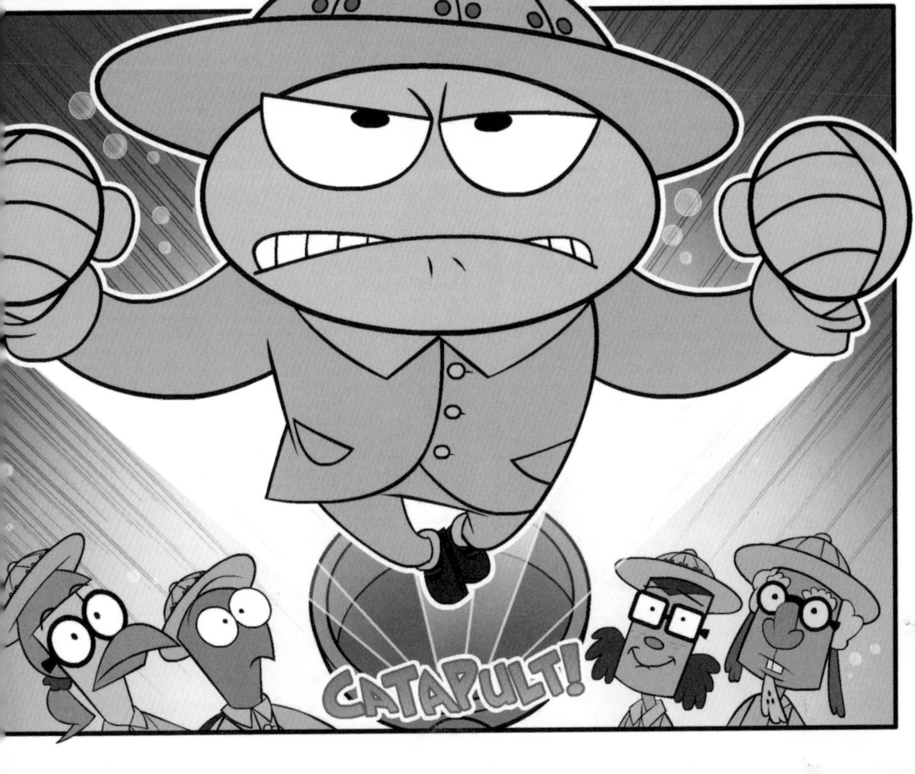
CATAPULT!

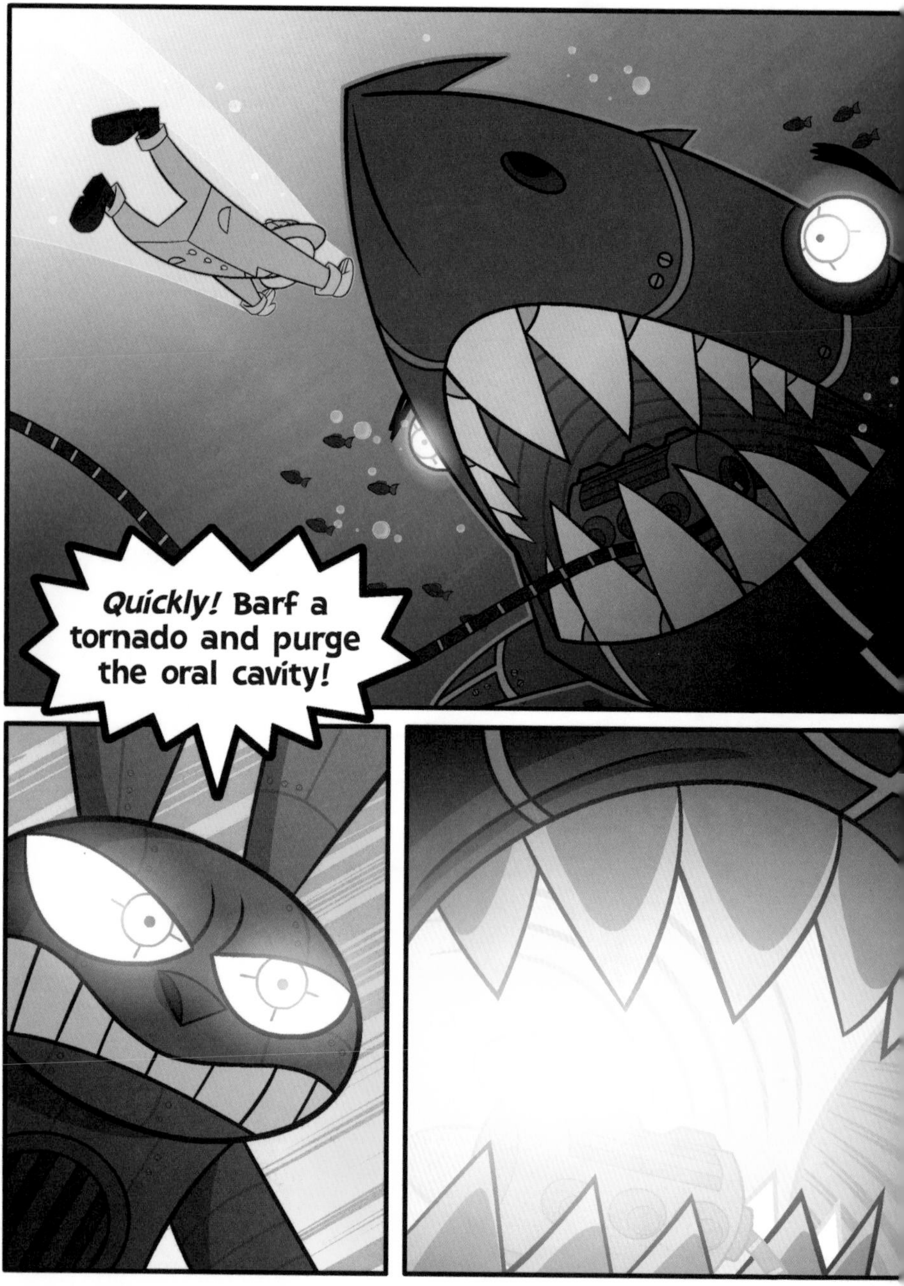
Quickly! Barf a tornado and purge the oral cavity!

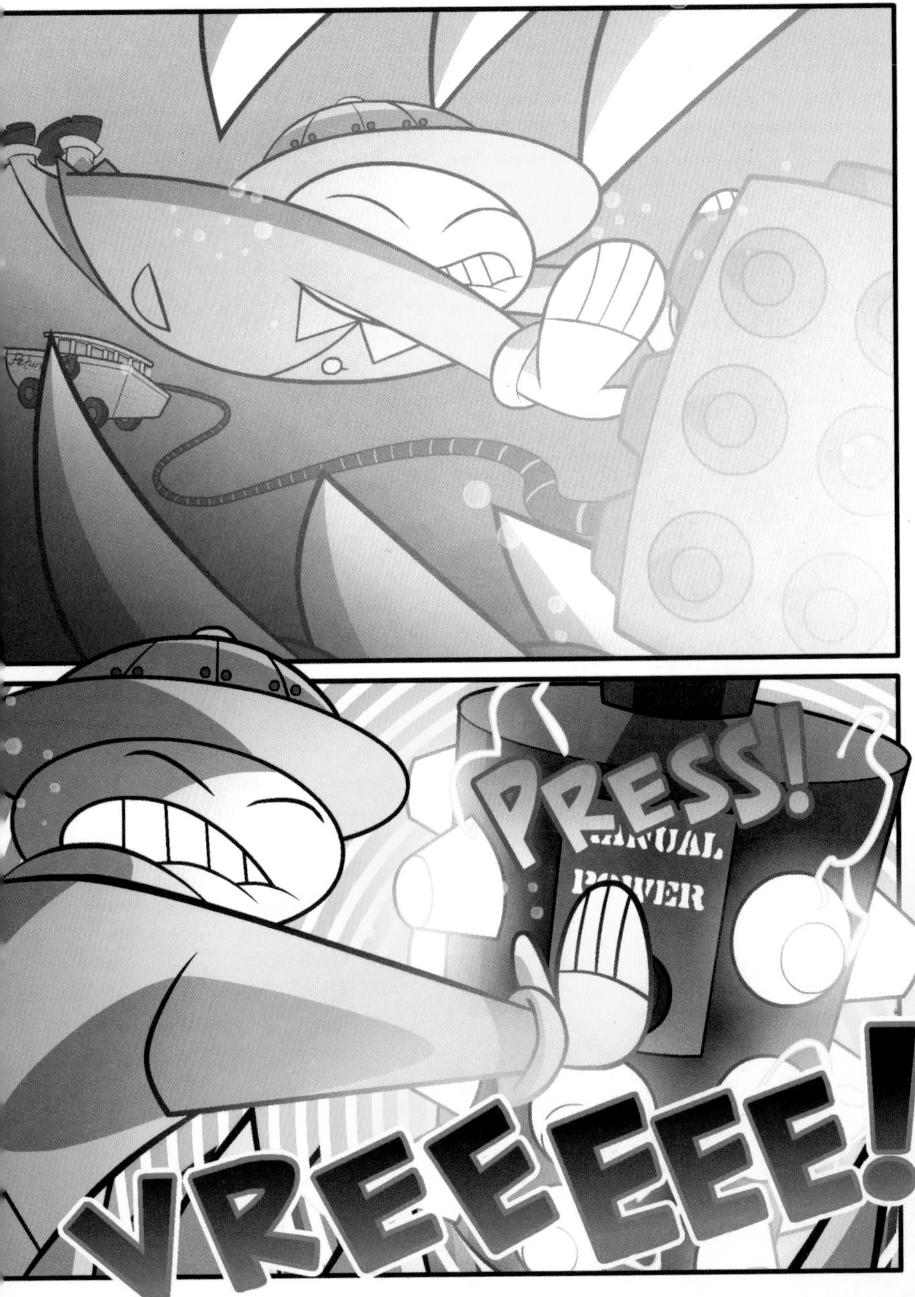

PRESS!
VREEEEE!

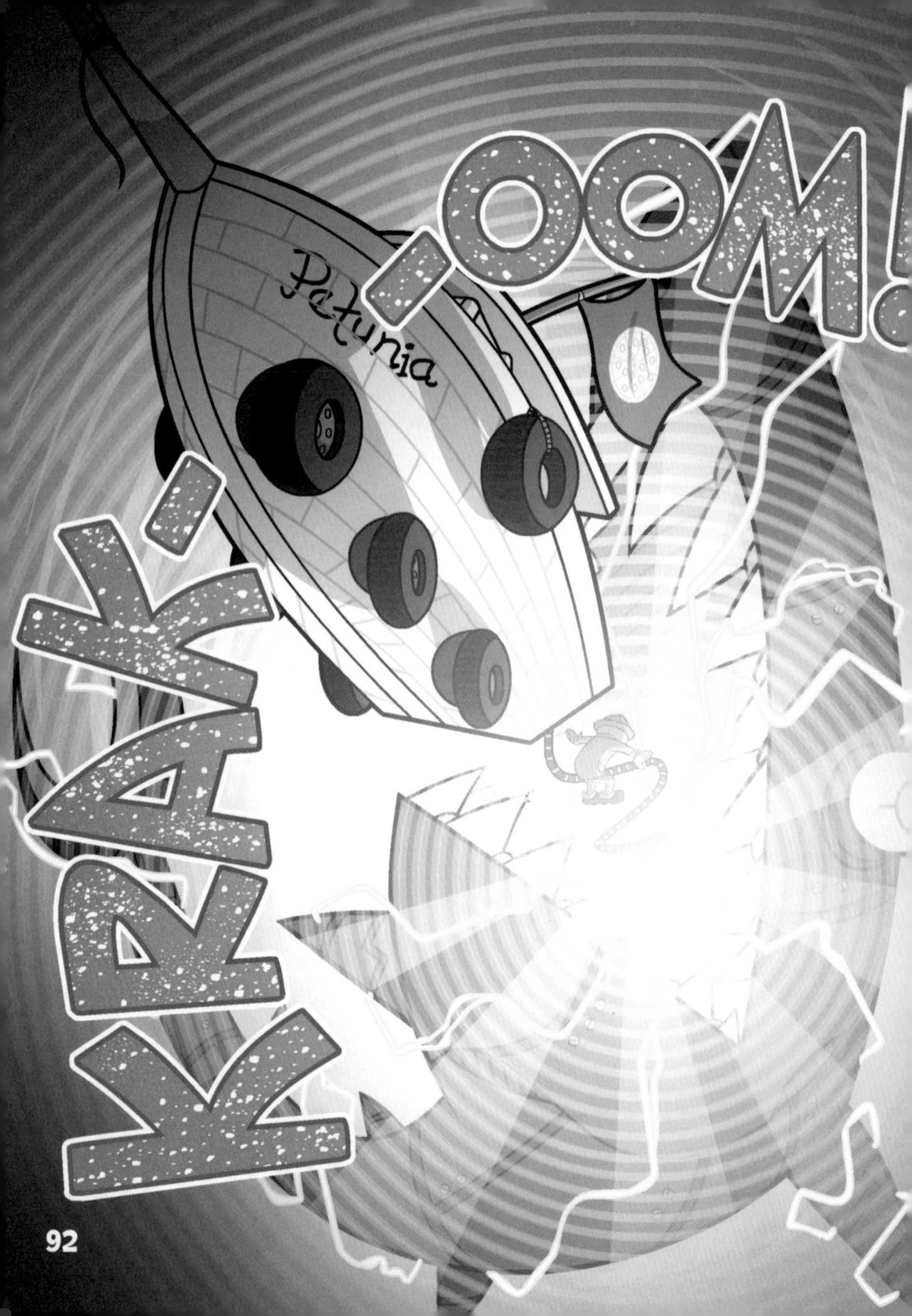
KRAK-OOM!
Petunia

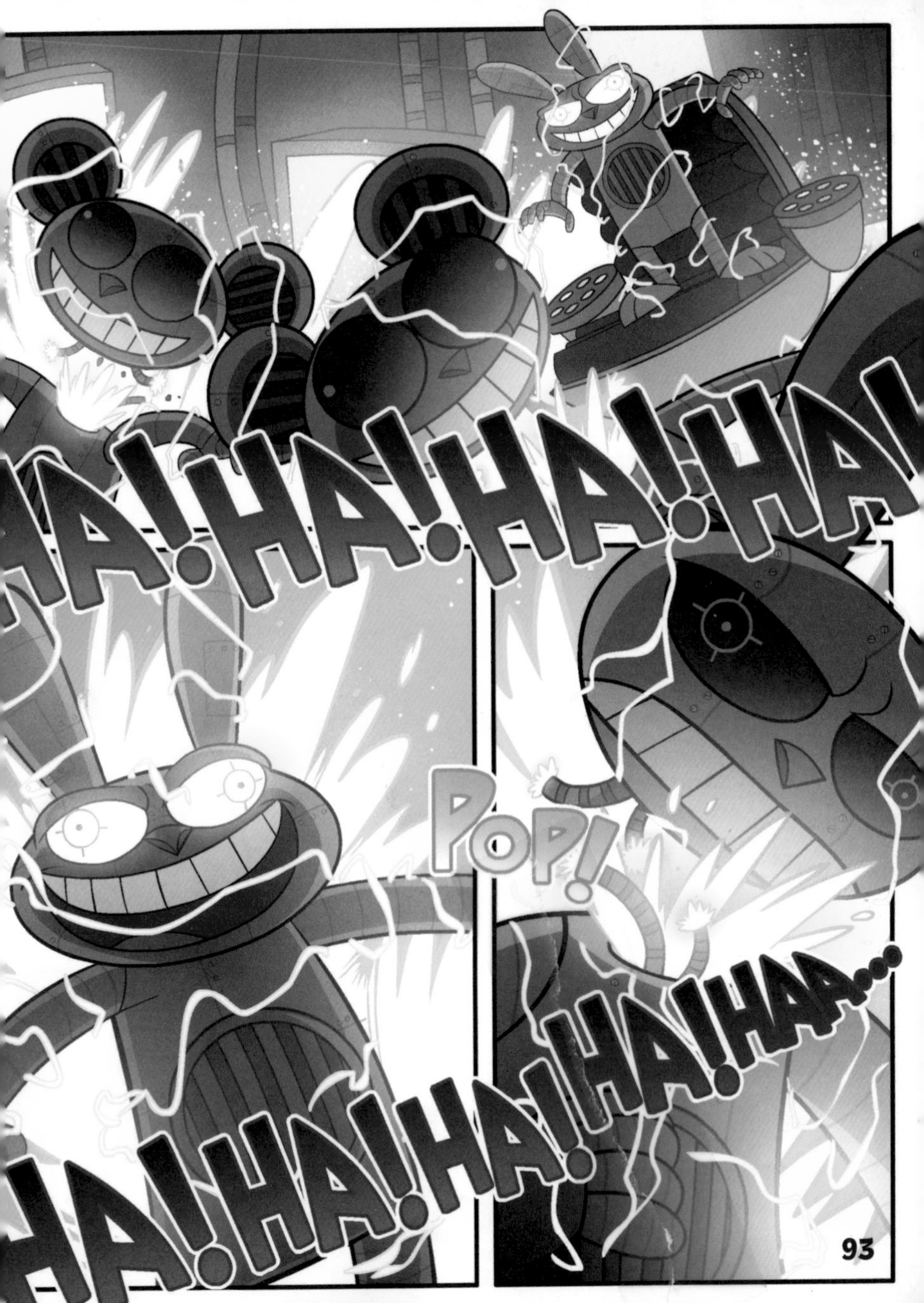
HA!HA!HA!HA!HA!HA!
POP!
HA!HA!HA!HA!HA!HAA...

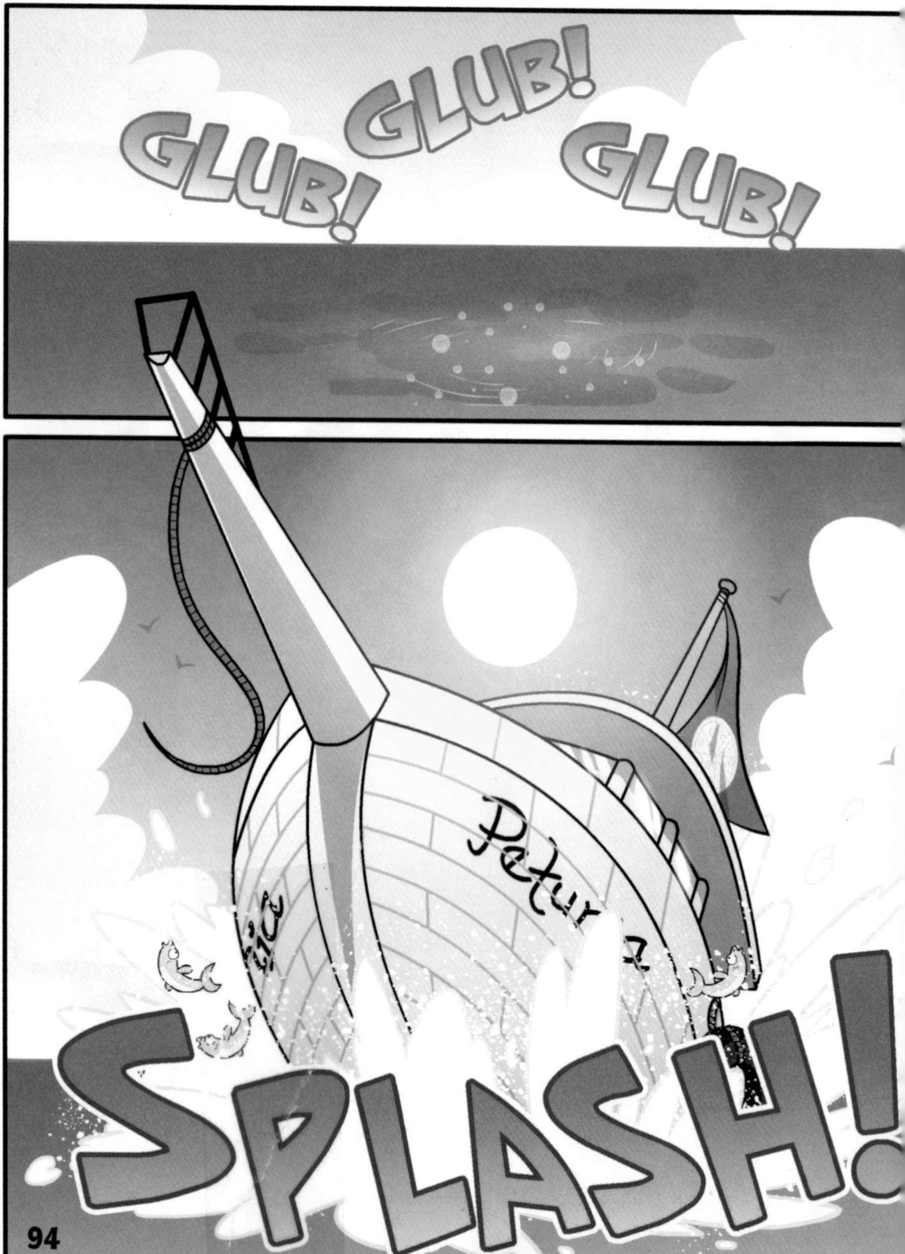
GLUB! GLUB! GLUB!
SPLASH!

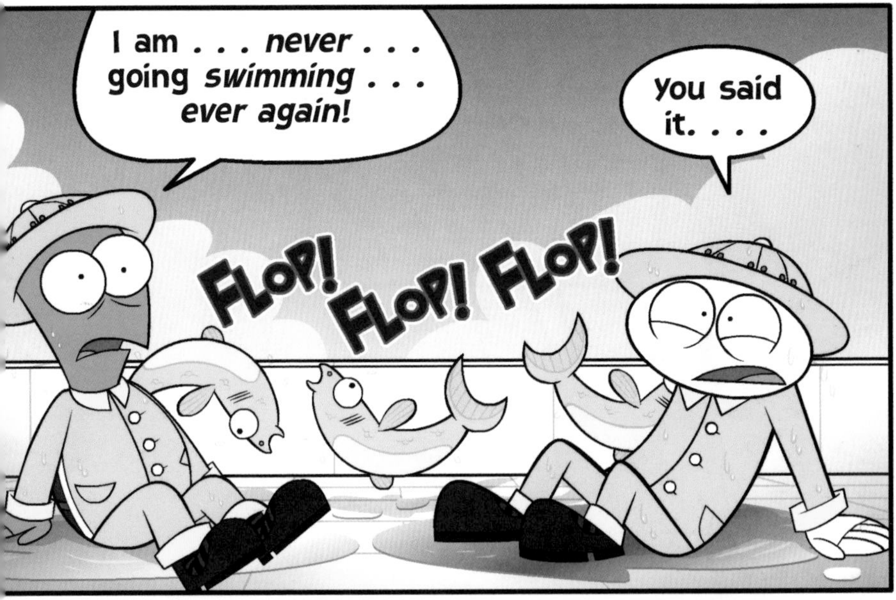
I am . . . *never* . . . going *swimming* . . . *ever again!*
You said it. . . .
FLOP! FLOP! FLOP!

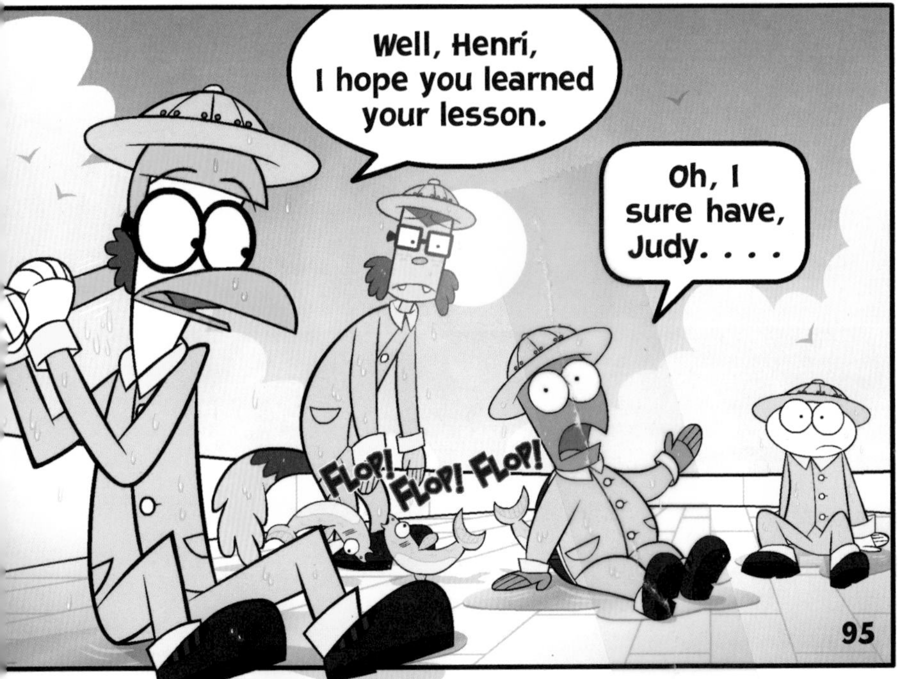
Well, Henri, I hope you learned your lesson.
Oh, I sure have, Judy. . . .
FLOP! FLOP! FLOP!

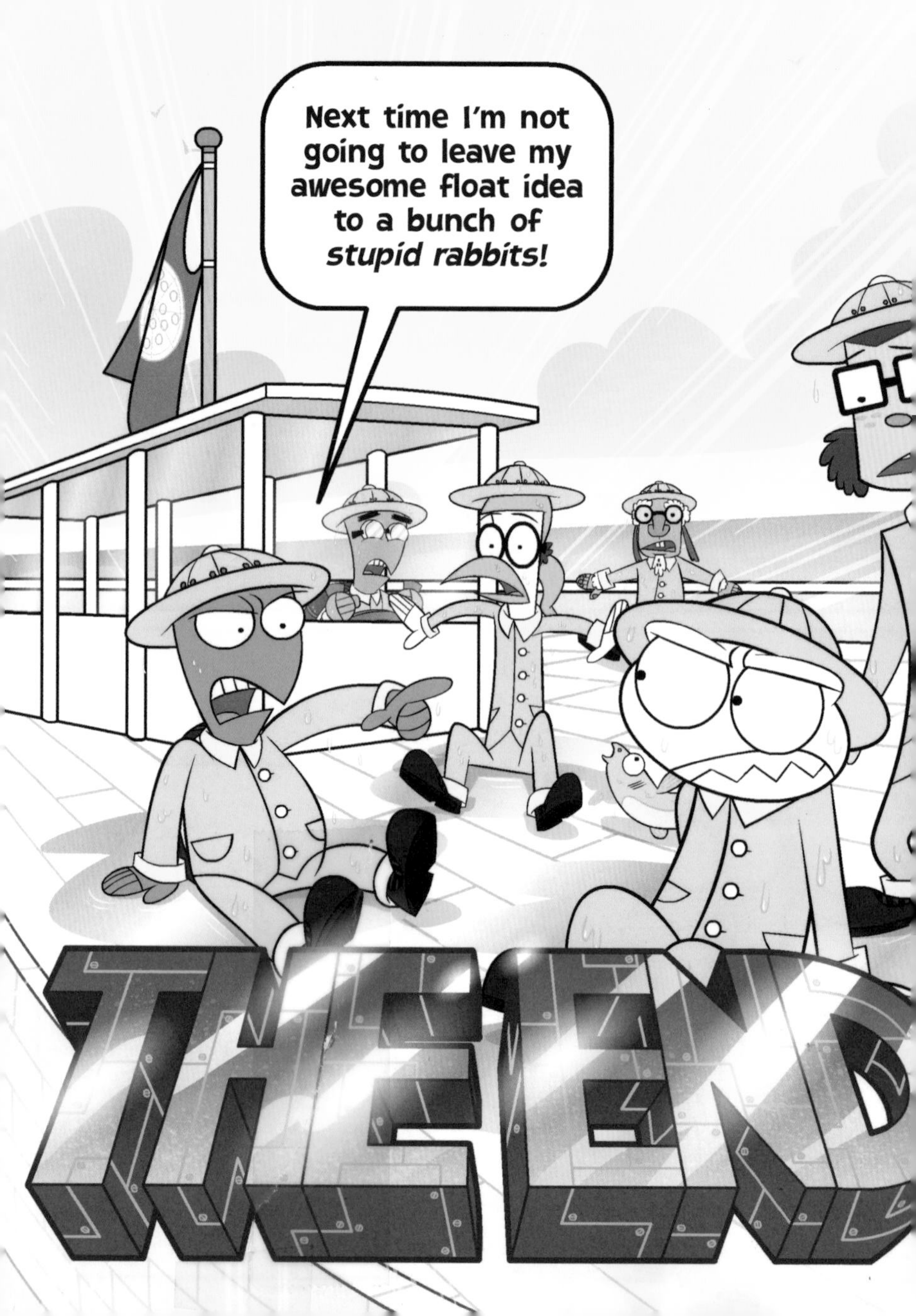
Next time I'm not going to leave my awesome float idea to a bunch of *stupid rabbits!*
THE END